JASON ROPER

J. ALSPAUGH

Printed in the United States of America

First Printing 2025

ISBN-13: 978-1-966775-06-5

DEDICATION

To my wonderfully supportive family and Christina Levy for their involvement in the writing and production of this book.

Jason Roper Book Series

PROLOGUE

She watched, helpless, as the pale liquid flowed from the syringe into her son's bloodstream. "That seems like an awful lot," she worried aloud.

The man injected the last of the fluid and then turned to face her. He put a hand on her shoulder and squeezed it gently. "He's fine, Mary. I studied it out very carefully and didn't give him a drop more than was necessary."

"He's so little." She reached out to stroke the little boy's dark hair. "Are you sure we are doing the right thing?"

He put the syringe down and pressed a bit of cotton onto the boy's arm. "Hand me a Band-Aid."

She obeyed. "He's only three, Nathan. Maybe we should have…"

"He's fine." The words were spoken firmly and Mary fell silent.

Nathan put the Band-Aid over the cotton and then started putting away the items that lay around the small body on the table. "The gestation period should be exactly 15 years," he told her, excitement lingering in his voice. "He'll be 18 years old, and he'll be a hero like no other."

She merely nodded, not sharing his enthusiasm.

"Meanwhile, I'll analyze the original compound and in a few years I'll be able to reproduce 8/15. I'll work on speeding up the gestation period…" He was muttering now, more to himself than the woman standing silently beside him. "If only

Ellerton had recorded the formula he used before his death."

"What will you do with it when you reproduce it?" she asked startling him out of his reverie.

"Sell it, of course." He put his hands on her shoulders. "Honey, if this goes like I've planned, we'll be set for the rest of our lives, and his." He gestured at the boy and went back to his work. "There are people, big people, who will pay plenty for this." He held up a small beaker of pale liquid.

"And they will make other people invincible?" she asked.

"Yes. But they will pay big for it." He grinned as he returned the precious beaker to its place inside the sturdy cabinet. He closed the door, pulled out a key ring, and locked it. Tugging on the door handles to make sure it was secure.

"But what if the people you sell it to use it to make criminals?" Mary asked, her brow creased with worry.

"I think the 'good guys' will be willing to pay a pretty penny to keep it out of their hands." He smiled and patted the locked cabinet door. "I'll start on it tomorrow."

"Don't you care that you could be making unstoppable villains?" she asked.

"I'll offer it to the right people first." He caught himself and looked at her "Don't worry about it. I think we'll be pretty busy raising our own little hero to worry about petty things like that. Besides, in 15 years he'll be invincible, so it won't matter if there are unstoppable villains because they won't be able to hurt our boy." He gently slid his arms under the boy's limp body and lifted him from the table. "He'll be the best hero this world has ever known."

"The rest of the people won't be invincible, Nathan." Mary told him bluntly and he shot her a warning look.

"Drop it, Mary. I'll worry about the selling. I don't want to hear any more about it from you."

She stood silent; if he had slapped her it would have had the same effect. Her eyes were hard as she watched him walk toward the door. She glanced at the cabinet then pulled a little toy train from her pocket and set it on the counter beside an empty beaker. Her mouth was set in a thin determined line as she followed him out the door.

"Pull the door shut after you and make sure it locks." He told her and she obeyed. She opened the back door for him, then gave a little exasperated groan.

"What now?" He asked still holding the boy in his arms.

"His train. I left it inside somewhere."

"We can get it tomorrow." He was trying to figure out the best way to get the limp body of his son into the little car seat.

"We won't get a moment's peace without it," she warned.

"Fine, go get it. But hurry." He turned so she could unclip the key ring from his belt loop. "Don't leave the keys."

"I won't." She hurried to the door and let herself in, pulling it closed behind her. She grabbed the train and stuffed it back into her pocket before making a beeline for the forbidden cabinet. Her fingers were steady as she unlocked the door and pulled the beaker from the shelf. She placed it on the table then returned to the cabinet. Her eyes quickly scanned the various glass containers coming to rest on a small jar of white powder. She glanced at the door as she pulled on a rubber lab glove. Opening the jar she took a pinch of the powder and carefully added it to the precious liquid careful not to get any on the sides of the glass. She watched as the powder dissolved into the irreplaceable compound, the change in color was hardly perceptible. She smiled, satisfied, and deftly removed the glove, pulling it inside out and placing it deep into her other pocket. She could not afford to leave any evidence. She replaced the jar and compound exactly as she had found them and locked the cabinet. She tested it to make sure it was secure, and then hurried for the door.

"What took you so long?" Nathan demanded. The car was hot and he was beginning to perspire.

"I'm sorry," she handed him the keys and he started the car. She looked back at her baby; still sleeping soundly from the mild anesthetic he had been given.

"He won't even know it happened." Nathan reassured her, his tone was gentle now.

"I know." She answered but did not look at her husband as they pulled away from the lab.

"Just think, he'll be a hero, he'll save thousands of lives." He reached over and patted her hand. "We did it for him."

She nodded, her eyes knowing. She had done the right thing, and she had done it for him.

ONE

"Patrick?"

The dark-haired teenager glanced at the hands of the clock on the wall. It was a little past nine. "In here, Kirk." Patrick called, turning his attention back to his laptop.

Kirk pushed the door open and it banged against the wall. "You have a letter."

"Do you mind putting it on my desk?" Patrick asked without looking up from the screen.

"I could." Kirk answered, leaning against the door frame.

The bitterness in his tone caught Patrick's attention and he looked up at his friend. "Okay?"

"If you look closely it says urgent." Kirk drew out the word tracing it with his finger so Patrick could see.

"Fine, give it to me." Patrick's tone was annoyed. He set his computer aside and slid his legs off the bed. "I don't know why you have to do this with every letter my dad sends."

Kirk tapped the letter gently on his open hand ignoring the look Patrick gave him. "I was wondering." Kirk's green eyes were serious. "Why is it your dad always sends urgent letters? I mean he's only been gone a month."

"Maybe he's in a hurry." Patrick rose and took the letter from Kirk.

"Urgent and priority? Something's up. As usual."

"Well, I can't say you personally delivering our mail is normal either." Patrick answered sitting on the bed again.

"I mean, it's not like we go to the post office, we do have a mail box outside just like everyone else."

"It said urgent."

"They all do, Kirk." Patrick laid the letter on his desk.

"You're not going to open it?"

Patrick rolled his eyes in exasperation. "Kirk, they always say urgent and I never open them until you leave. This isn't a new process. I don't see why you feel you need to go snooping through my mail."

Kirk crossed his arms. "You think you can keep this all a secret don't you? I'm not exactly blind, Patrick."

"Not exactly." Patrick agreed.

Kirk glared at him. "You just laze around while the rest of us have to get side jobs and work our tails off. Have you looked at the time? Oh, I forgot, you don't like clocks." He sneered, "Some of the guys think you have some sort of clock-a-phobia."

Patrick glared back. "What's new? You guys have been talking behind my back for years. And for your information I am very aware of the time. That circular object on the wall is called a clock." Patrick returned his attention to his computer. "Its 9:15 and I'm studying."

Kirk toyed with the model car on Patrick's desk. "Medicine or news?" His tone was bored.

"Medicine." Patrick knew what was coming. "I'm studying for my final exam, which happens to be tomorrow."

"That's all you do now, study. Remember when we were 17? You were normal…"

"We used to hang out and do things together." Patrick finished.

"Well we did." Kirk was annoyed by Patrick's tone. "We used to be friends. Now all you do is study. Why do you think I deliver these?" Kirk asked, picking up the letter again. "Because it is the only time I get to see you."

"Kirk, I really am sorry, but you knew this was going to happen. I have to get my EMT certification finished up and I'm already a month behind schedule. Besides, I did a lot of extra classes and studying last year, too."

"Patrick, you're eighteen, lighten up."

"I am painfully aware of my age, Kirk. I was supposed to have this all done by the thirtieth of April."

"Why is April so special? Your birthday was in August."

"Okay, what if you come work out with me? We could spend some time together and…stuff."

Kirk rolled his eyes. "Yeah, just like the last time."

"Something unexpected came up."

"Save it for the jury." Kirk told him with an angry glare. "You could have called and let me know. That's the fifth time you've stood me up."

"Oh, you've been counting, huh?" Patrick met his angry eyes. "Well, Kirk, there are some things that are just out of my control."

"I've had it up to here with your excuses, Patrick." Kirk held his hand over his head to show the level of his frustration. "It's been almost a month since we've even talked. You don't even know what is going on anymore."

"I do too." Patrick defended. "You're hanging out with a bunch of lowlifes."

"So, now my friends are lowlifes?"

"They're thieving gangsters, Kirk. You can't go down much further than that."

Kirk's eyes narrowed, his look was hateful. "You'd better watch what you say, Patrick. It doesn't take much to get on their hit list."

Patrick was not scared or impressed. "Listen Kirk, you drop them and I'll make time to hang out with you."

Kirk hesitated and Patrick could tell he was not buying it. "When?"

Patrick squinted up at the corner of the room as if his schedule were written there. "Tuesday?"

Kirk was ready to play his trump card. "Why," he tossed the letter back onto the desk, and folded his arms. "Do you not travel on Tuesdays?"

Patrick's brown eyes met Kirk's, and Kirk could tell he was caught off guard. "What do you mean?"

"I know about your 'mysterious' trips. We've been keeping an eye on you?"

"We...?"

Kirk leaned his shoulder against the wall. "Don't try to deny it, Patrick."

Kirk seemed to have grown into a man overnight. Patrick had known their friendship had been waning, and that Kirk had taken his lack of free time as a personal insult. But for the first time, Patrick realized his childhood friend could be a threat to everything he had worked for all these years.

"I'm not trying to deny anything." Patrick was thinking fast, but he could see no way out. "Everyone goes on a trip now and then."

"Sure." Kirk kept his arms folded. "I mean, look at me."

"Come on, Kirk, What's the big deal?"

Kirk's eyes were hard. "The big deal, Patrick, is that before you turned eighteen, I was your best friend, we hung out, talked, and shared our dreams. Then suddenly you drop me and become a whole new person..."

"I have been planning on taking this course for forever, I couldn't get the certificate or a job in medicine until I was eighteen. I told you that before."

"Yeah well, you studied before for it and still had a life. Now you've stopped hanging out with the guys and won't go to anything with us. You got busy on your birthday but you changed in April. Now you keep to yourself like some hermit with a secret life. You are some sort of hot shot, living it up like a millionaire. I don't even know you anymore."

Patrick was silent. It crushed him to lose his friend, but he had a mission he could not go back on. He was no longer an ordinary teenage boy, but he could not tell Kirk that. "Kirk...I..."

Kirk waited, he could tell Patrick was thinking hard and fast.

"I can't..."Patrick shrugged. "I don't know what to say. I'm sorry, but there are some things I can't change."

"Sure," Kirk smoothed his red hair, his movements were controlled. "You got your life, I got mine." He turned and left the room without another word.

Patrick waited until he heard the front door close, then picked up the letter from his dad. He hesitated for a moment before opening it. Unfolding the letter, he laid the airline ticket aside. He had been on trips for training before, but this was different, this was his first real mission.

———

Patrick closed his suitcase and clicked the lock in place. His mom, a tall, pretty woman with straight dark hair and warm brown eyes, came into his room and handed him a sandwich and an apple.

"In case you get hungry on the way." She smiled but Patrick could tell she was worried.

"I'll be fine, Mom." He reassured her, taking the food and putting it into his backpack. He was scared, but he could not let her see it. What if his Dad's invention had not worked? Patrick shook his head to clear it.

"Are you okay?" his mom asked softly.

He met her eyes and managed a weak smile. "I'm a little nervous."

She hugged him tightly. "You have every right to be nervous," she whispered. They stood there a moment then she stepped back and looked into his eyes. "I'll be praying for you."

"Thanks, Mom." He slipped the ticket into the front pocket of his backpack. "I guess we'd better go."

She nodded, "Are there any last instructions?"

Patrick laughed softly. "Yeah, make sure you feed that dog I don't have."

She smiled back. "Consider him fed." She picked up his backpack and grunted. "Patrick McCard, this thing weighs a ton! You are going to break your back. What's in here?"

"Some books of mine and a few of Dad's he wanted me to bring."

"It feels like you packed the library."

"I'll get it." He swung it onto his shoulder and grinned at her. "I've been working out remember."

She just shook her head. "Don't come crying to me when your back..." she looked at him and fell silent.

"I guess you don't have to worry about that anymore, Mom." he said, trying to lighten the mood. He could tell she was holding back her tears.

"You always were my little dare devil. Always coming back skinned up from your latest adventure with Kirk."

Patrick nodded solemnly. "I guess it's all over now." There was a sadness in his voice. His eyes came to rest on the picture of him and Kirk that stood on his desk.

"You miss him, don't you?"

"Yeah, I do."

"Are you sorry we chose this for you?" she asked softly.

"No" He looked away from the picture. "It needed to be done. I'm proud you chose me."

She looked at him for a long time. "I love you, Patrick."

"I love you too, Mom."

"Alright, I guess it's now or never." She picked up the suitcase and Patrick took it from her.

"I'll be the porter, Mom. You can be the chauffer. "

"That's a deal."

Once the bags were downstairs they quickly turned out all the houselights then slipped out in the darkness to the car. Patrick closed the trunk softly and moved to the passenger door. A movement in the shadow of the house caught his eye. He paused for a second before slipping into the car.

"What is it?" his mom asked. She had taken the precaution of turning off the dome light in the car.

"Someone's watching us."

"Do you have any idea who?"

"Yeah, I think it's Kirk." Patrick was ticked.

"But why would Kirk be spying on our house at two in the morning?"

"He says he knows about my trips. I guess he has been watching for a while now. Mom, what if he…goes off the deep end?" Patrick asked.

"You mean becomes an informer or something?"

"Or something. You'll be here alone and there is no telling what he will do."

"Honey, this is Kirk you are talking about. Not some villain."

"What time is it?"

She shrugged, "It was 2:30 when we came out."

"So I've got time." Patrick opened his door.

"For what?" She hissed at him. "Where are you going?"

"Lock the doors and wait for me." He shut his door and strode purposely toward the shadowy figure.

"Kirk, you've gone too far this time." Patrick's voice was low but carried well.

Kirk spun to go but Patrick had anticipated this and dove for his ankles, knocking him to the ground.

"Let go of me!" Kirk demanded.

Patrick grabbed the front of his shirt and hauled him

to his feet. "If I ever catch you spying on me or my family again…" Patrick spoke through clenched teeth, his eyes snapped with unbridled anger.

"What will you do?" Kirk spat back jerking himself free. "Make me sorry? You've already done that. I'm sorry I ever knew you. For years I thought our friendship was real and now I see it was just a diversion."

"What do you mean by that?" Patrick demanded.

"You were waiting for your big day. Planning and training for it, while I naively thought you were…human."

"Human?" Patrick rolled his eyes. "That's really rich, Kirk. Is that supposed to hurt? Because it doesn't. I'm doing what I have to do, and you…" Patrick jabbed Kirk in the chest and Kirk smacked his hand away.

"Keep your grimy mitts off me." Kirk interrupted. "Just because you have some high calling doesn't mean anything to me. You think you're somebody big. I could take you out in a minute, and you'd be sobbing for my mercy."

The anger drained out of Patrick. He knew exactly what Kirk was talking about. "You really would wouldn't you? You would hurt my parents just to get even?"

"Yeah, I've had enough of you and your 'studies.'" Kirk was still seething with anger. "If our friendship means so little to you, it means nothing to me."

"Kirk, why does it have to be this way?"

"You tell me, you chose it."

"I want to be very clear about this whole situation." Patrick took a deep breath. He no longer felt weak or scared. The situation called for firm strength on his part, and that is what he displayed. "Are you saying that we are no longer friends or that from now on we are enemies?" Kirk hesitated so Patrick went on. "You have the right to choose either way, but I need to know now what you have decided so that I can act accordingly."

"Do you have a gun on you?" Kirk asked.

"Do you actually think that I would pull a gun on you and kill you?" Patrick's anger swelled up once more. "You know me better than that."

"No, I don't know you at all anymore."

Patrick pulled his jacket open for Kirk to see. "I'm unarmed. Happy?"

Kirk hesitated still.

Patrick glanced around; he had the tingly feeling of being watched. It was all too clear to him now what Kirk meant to do. In the last week, Patrick had saved someone's life, crossing the neighborhood gang in the process. They did not know who he was and so he had been able to avoid them, but now Kirk had brought them right to his house.

"Kirk, I have the feeling you decided long before you came out tonight."

Kirk shifted a little under Patrick's searching eyes, but the anger had not left him. "You chose, not me. You chose this months ago when you decided I couldn't be trusted with your secret. I know a lot more than you think."

"It really doesn't matter what you know at this point," Patrick answered, but Kirk ignored him.

"I know you are leaving at 3:50. I know something changed in you on April 30th, exactly eight months and fifteen days after your eighteenth birthday. I know you don't like digital clocks for a reason other than preference. I also know that your Dad has been sending you updates, keeping you informed of your 'missions' as he assigns them." Kirk smiled. "You see, you thought you could be all secretive and hide it all from me. You thought I wasn't trustworthy. So here we are."

"You just proved you are not trustworthy. You might as well tell your friends to come out and face me. I don't have a lot of time to deal with them."

"You may not have time to deal with them, but you will

be dealing with me for a very long time."

"So, now you are some sort of sworn enemy of mine?" Patrick was not impressed.

"I won't give you the pleasure of a sure decision."

Patrick laughed coldly. "You couldn't have been more clear if you had shouted it through a megaphone. Goodbye Kirk. It was good knowing you."

"I wish I could say the same." Kirk turned to go. "He's yours now, I'm through with him."

Three burly men stepped out of the darkness. One pointed a gun at Patrick. "Someone would like to have a little visit with you."

"That's very nice, maybe some other time."

The man stepped toward Patrick threateningly. "I don't think I made myself clear."

Patrick lunged forward and struck the man hard. The gun went off, the bullet disappeared harmlessly into the thick grass as Patrick made a run for the car. He was suddenly grateful he had taken his father's advice to take up track. A shot rang out and Patrick felt as if someone had poked him in the back. It registered that he had been hit with a bullet and he stumbled as he reached the car. He did his best to imitate the actions of a wounded man as he scrambled into the running car and slammed the door.

"Keep low and step on it," Patrick commanded. She obeyed and they lurched forward.

"They shot you!" his mother gasped. She was hunched down, her eyes wild with fear.

"I know, keep down." A bullet ripped through the side window and exited through the windshield.

Mrs. McCard screamed.

"Mom, it's okay, we are doing fine."

"Patrick, they are trying to kill us." His mother's eyes were wide.

"I know, Mom." Patrick took the wheel from her. "You stay down and push the pedals I'll drive."

"What if you get shot?" she asked frantically.

"Nothing will happen." For a second their eyes met and she understood. He turned his attention back to the road just in time to avoid a large trash truck.

"So it worked," she whispered.

Patrick smiled. "I guess so. I am now officially invincible."

Two

They swerved through town at a breakneck pace; the gunman's car stayed right on their tail. Patrick knew that this was not just Kirk's little gang. Something bigger was involved.

Bullets tore through the back window and a few ricocheted off Patrick's head with no effect whatsoever.

"Does it hurt?" His mother asked holding on for dear life as they swerved through a side street. She had both feet on the gas.

"No, just feels like someone is poking me. Kind of annoying really." He paused to navigate through a tight place. "Mom, this really isn't going to work. I mean what are you going to do. I can't just go off on an airplane and leave you with all these thugs.

"I'll call your father. He'll send some people to take care of me and them." She reached for her purse.

He glanced behind them. "I don't see the car." He returned his attention to the street before him, looking between the cracks in the windshield. "Mom, we're slowing down!"

"Stay calm. They can't hurt you."

"It's not me I'm concerned about," Patrick informed her "It's you."

"Then let's switch places so I can call." She stepped on the brakes and Patrick steered them to the side of the road.

"What if they pull me over? Dad told me not to bring my license." Patrick reminded her.

"And what you were doing was legal?" She shoved him toward the door. "Get around quick before they catch up."

He jumped out of the car and ran around to the driver's side and clambered in. Without hesitation he put the car in gear and pushed the gas.

"I was well aware of the high speed driving lessons your father gave you on your father-son outings." She smiled, but he could tell she was still shaken. "You know, Patrick, you are a perfect hero."

He laughed. "Thanks, Mom."

Mr. McCard directed them to an old warehouse where, when they pulled up, four men appeared and quickly transferred Patrick's luggage to another car. Patrick and his mom were directed to take the back seats of the heavily tinted car. They obeyed and soon were off again. This time a sharp man who looked like he belonged in the secret service was behind the wheel. Another man, who reminded Patrick of a Navy Seal, sat in the passenger seat. A lady who was much younger than his mother sat on the other side of Mrs. McCard by the outside window.

They pulled to a stop and the Navy Seal grabbed the baggage from the trunk. The young lady walked beside Mrs. McCard as they entered the airport. Patrick noticed that they were scanning the crowds and were very aware of anyone even remotely close by. They said their goodbyes under close supervision and Patrick boarded the 3:50 flight to "Destination Unknown". The obvious code created by Mr. McCard.

———

When he arrived, a man in a sharp looking suit approached Patrick as he walked off the plane.

"Are you the one?" the man asked. His voice was deep and serious.

Patrick looked around. "Which one?"

The man looked a little annoyed. "The one I'm here for."

"That depends on who you were sent to meet. I mean honestly, how am I supposed to know if I'm the one you came for or not." Patrick had had a lot of time to think on the plane ride and he was still riled about Kirk endangering his mom just to get even. He was in no mood for cheesy secrecy.

"Do you know the code?"

"Morris code, prisoner's code, the code to the bike chain, I got them covered."

The man was not amused. "Mr. McCard sent me to pick up a…" the man pulled a business card from his pocket and read from the back: "young man wearing a brown leather jacket with a flight emblem on the front." You got the jacket, you must be him."

"Good thing I didn't get hot on the plane." Patrick muttered.

"What is your name?"

"I don't think I'm authorized to give it to you." His father had not told him what to expect when he arrived. The gaps in the communication between Patrick and Mr. McCard had been becoming more frequent as the months dragged on. The letter with the airplane tickets had been the first contact with his dad since he had left on his last trip. Every other time his dad had met him in the main terminal.

"Suit yourself. You have any bags?"

"One."

"Let's get it and go."

"Wait." Patrick shifted his back pack on his shoulders. "I have no idea who you are or who you work for."

"I told you, I work for Mr. McCard."

"Where's your proof?"

"You were born at 8:15 on 8/15."

"That much you could have learned by reading public records."

He looked exasperated and pulled out his cell phone. "Mr.

McCard? Yes, Sir. I found him but he's asking for proof…yes I know sir but…Alright, we will be by carousel three. Yes… thank you, Sir." He closed the phone and looked at Patrick. "I hope you are satisfied. He is coming in. "

"Then let's get to carousel three."

————

Mr. McCard was the kind of man that catches your eye and makes you wonder if he were a spy or a member of the FBI. He stood straight; his five foot eight form topped with dark hair which was graying around the edges. His perfect hair was combed to the side and there was not a wrinkle in his neatly pressed suit. His eyes met Patrick's, and Patrick could see by the twinkle in his brown eyes that his father was pleased to see him.

"Welcome." Mr. McCard held out his hand and Patrick shook it firmly.

"Thank you, Mr. McCard."

"Have you found your bags?"

"Yes, Sir, I only have the one."

"Good, then let's be off." He strode toward the exit and Patrick grabbed his bag to follow. "Let Mr. Taroe get your bag. He is a capable man."

Patrick glanced at Taroe, standing there in his pressed suit and set the bag down. "I can get it."

"No, I will get your bag." Mr. Taroe was stiffly professional.

"Thank you, Mr. Taroe."

Without a word Taroe picked up the bag and strode after Mr. McCard with Patrick tagging along behind.

————

"This will be your room. I hope it is acceptable."

"Looks fine to me." Patrick looked around the room. There was nothing fancy about it, just a little room with a full bed and hotel type furniture. "Mr. Taroe, when do I meet with Mr. McCard?"

"At two sharp. I will be here at 1:45 to pick you up. I was instructed to tell you to get some rest while you can."

"Great, thanks for all your help."

"My pleasure, Sir." Mr. Taroe pulled the door closed behind him as he left the room.

Patrick grinned, bowing to the door. "My pleasure, Sir. Have a restful afternoon, I shall see you at tea." He shook his head. "I wonder where they picked him up." He set his bag on the bed and went to the window. He was glad they had put him on the second floor so he could use the window as an exit if he needed to. The view was like the room, nothing fancy, just streets and buildings and tangled roads. He sighed and went back to the bed flopping down on it without bothering to pull back the covers.

———

A knock at the door woke Patrick from a sound sleep. He glanced at his watch and leapt out of bed. It was 1:50 and the firm knock was probably an irritated Mr. Taroe.

"I'm on my way," Patrick called trying to straighten his rumpled clothing. He turned on the faucet, splashed a handful of water on his hair, and did his best to smooth it down. He grabbed his backpack and room key and flung open the door. There stood Mr. Taroe. The chauffer looked him over from his dripping hair to his untied shoe and shook his head.

"I'm really sorry, Mr. Taroe," Patrick apologized, following the chauffer to the exit a few doors down. "I fell asleep and…" he stopped, realizing the older man already knew what had happened. Following Taroe, he said nothing more, and climbed silently into the back of the black car that waited outside. Taroe started the car and pulled away from the curb.

Patrick rummaged through his backpack and found a

comb. Running the comb through his wet hair, he parted it using his reflection in the tinted window.

"Mr. Taroe?"

"Yes?" Taroe's tone said clearly he did not want to talk, but Patrick pressed on.

"Why do chauffeurs get the whole front to themselves?"

"Because they don't always want to socialize with those they are transporting."

"Hmm. I never thought of it that way. Have you always been a chauffer?"

"No."

"Does anything exciting ever happen while you are driving for Mr. McCard?"

"No."

"I would think you would have some cool stories since Mr. McCard is a very interesting person."

Silence.

"So, the passengers never get to sit up front?"

"No."

"So, I guess celebrities are just like little kids. Neither can sit up front." Patrick leaned back. "So how come you don't like me?"

"I am a chauffer. My job is to get you from point A to point B. Not to entertain you on the way."

"I know, but I can tell we really didn't hit it off. And if you are going to be driving me it would be nice to know that at least the chauffer is on my side."

Mr. Taroe didn't respond.

"Well, if I get in a jam at least I know who not to call." Patrick looked out the window at the passing cars and buildings and wondered how his mother was. He sighed involuntarily and checked the rear view mirror to make sure Mr. Taroe had not heard.

The chauffer's eyes flicked back to the road ahead, but

Patrick knew he had been watching.

THREE

They pulled to a stop in front of a large building that looked just like all the others standing around it. Its glass windows reflected the clouds that drifted lazily through the pale blue sky.

Patrick hopped out before Mr. Taroe and swung his backpack onto his shoulder. "Where do I meet him?"

"Room 903," Taroe replied.

"Thanks."

Patrick sprinted up the steps then attempted once more to smooth his clothing before entering the huge glass doors.

"Welcome to M.C. enterprises. May I help you?" The receptionist asked cheerfully.

"I have an appointment with Mr. McCard, should I just go up?"

"I will need to see your I.D."

"Um… well. I don't actually have it yet."

"You don't have an I.D. card?" She looked a little suspicious.

"No, not exactly."

"What do you mean by not exactly?"

"Couldn't you just give him a call?"

"Mr. McCard is a very busy man." She was trying to catch the eye of someone behind him. Patrick turned to look and saw a security guard.

"Sir." Patrick called.

The security guard looked up.

"The receptionist needs you."

The guard came over. "What is it, Milly?"

Milly's face flushed crimson. "This young man would like to see Mr. McCard, but he says he has no I.D."

"That could pose a problem. When was your meeting?"

"Two o'clock sharp. But I was a little late."

"How about I check…" a buzz from the receptionist's desk interrupted him.

She hurried over to the little box and pressed a button. "Yes, Mr. McCard?"

"Is there a young man down there? I had a meeting with him and he has not shown up yet."

"Yes, Mr. McCard, he is here. I'll send him right up."

"Thank you, Milly."

She looked up at Patrick. "You may go right up."

"Thank you."

He took the elevator to the 9th floor and easily found room 903. It was spacious and commanded a view of the entire city.

"Patrick, you finally made it." McCard enveloped him in a hug. "I was starting to worry about you."

"I overslept a bit then got stopped by your people downstairs," Patrick explained, taking the chair his father offered him. "Dad, we really need to think through this whole security thing because I don't know any of your people and they don't know me and I don't even know what name I should give them because I obviously can't be Patrick McCard…"

"Slow down, Son," McCard laughed, taking the chair across from him. "Let's deal with them one at a time."

Patrick leaned back and sighed. "I'm sorry, Dad."

"Don't beat yourself up over it, you have had a long day." McCard rose and pulled a box from behind his desk. "This should solve all those problems." He set it on the desk and Patrick came to inspect it. He pulled out an identification card. On the front was his picture and description and the word "approved" was in the place of a name.

"So I have to go by 'approved' now?" Patrick was not excited about the prospect.

"No, Patrick I just had to put that so you could get in. Have you come up with the name you want?"

"I figured my alias could be Hues Roper."

"That's different. How did you come up with that?

Patrick looked a little embarrassed. "It's the word 'superhero' mixed up, which is kinda lame but it was the best I could come up with so far."

"I think it's clever, a very different approach."

"Is that a dumb name?" Patrick asked. "I like Roper better than Hues. I could just go by Roper."

"No, it's not dumb at all, I think it's ingenious." McCard dropped the identification card into the shredder. "I'll have a new one made for you. What about your name when you are …the hero."

"I don't know, Dad. The only thing I have decided about that is I don't want to wear tights."

McCard laughed heartily. "I am glad to hear that." He assured Patrick when he caught his breath. "I've had clothes made up for you already."

"Great. You know how you made this jacket out of whatever that bullet resistant stuff is? Well, I got shot leaving home and it worked like a charm."

"Patrick, it's not bullet resistant. The clothing I have for you has been exposed to a very diluted solution of 8/15. I have tried many times to reproduce the compound I gave to you, without success. This solution is the closest I could get and seems to have no effect on the human body at all. The jacket you have was the first try at it and as you can see had a few errors." McCard pointed to a bullet hole in the lining of the jacket Patrick wore.

"Well, however it works it was great."

"Your Mom told me about it. I'm sorry about Kirk."

"I'd rather not talk about him just yet, Dad. I need some time to sort it all out."

"I understand. However, I believe these items will be of better quality and more resistant to both the impact of bullets and a certain amount of heat. If the bullet cannot travel more than an inch into the cloth it will not tear. So if I were wearing your clothes the bullet would go right through it because it would go right through me. But since the bullet cannot go through you, it cannot go through the clothes." McCard pulled a pair of black cargo pants from the box. How's this to replace the tights?"

"Wow, that's great! Is this really my suit?" Patrick took the pants and held them up to admire them.

"Half of it." McCard reached in again. "It also includes a nice black shirt. I was able to make you three shirts and two pair of cargos by diluting the compound." He laid the folded items out on the desk. "Like I said there is no way to reproduce it yet so this is all you have to work with. But don't worry, I am still working to descipher and recreate the compound. It is only a matter of time before you can have all the gear you want." McCard's eyes shone with the possibilities and for a moment he fell silent, lost in thought. He blinked and looked at Patrick again. "Right, and then of course there is the mask."

"Not the whole head 'you look like a creep' kind, right?"

McCard laughed, "No, I knew how you felt about that. I thought about going for the sunglasses look but that would cut off your peripheral vision. This is the simple 'put over your eyes' kind." He held it up to his face, "See, kind of like the Zorro look."

"Not bad." Patrick took the mask and slipped it over his head and down over his eyes. "How do I look?"

"It's crooked, but you'll get the hang of it."

"I don't get how this one little strip across my face makes it so no one can tell who I am. I mean, it's not like I changed anything."

"People will see what they want to. Besides even if they knew who you were, it wouldn't change anything. It's not like you have any weakness or can be hurt in any way."

"True, but the ones I love can be."

McCard smiled sadly. "You're a good kid."

"So I guess I'll have to be the Boy in Black or the B.I.B."

"You want to be known as bib?"

"No, not really." Patrick walked to the huge window and looked out. "I want something kinda cool sounding. I like the word sphere but I don't really know how it goes with saving people or anything."

"I think you are on the right track. Keep thinking; it will come to you."

"I could be called Cargo, 'cause of the pants."

McCard tried to hold back his amusement. "We'll sleep on it and see if we like it in the morning." McCard's face grew serious again. "Patrick, I have a few other things for you to take with you."

"Okay," Patrick looked curious.

McCard pulled a handgun from the box. "This is a Glock 23." He pulled a clip out of his desk drawer and slid it into place before handing it to Patrick.

Patrick took it carefully and tested its weight in his hand. "It's nice. Just like the one they had at the range."

"It is the one from at the range. You were practicing with this gun so you would know it inside and out when this time came."

"No wonder it fits so nice." Patrick sighted down the barrel.

"Patrick, I'd rather you didn't blow out the windows on your first visit."

Patrick lowered the gun and grinned. "Sorry, Dad. The gun's perfect."

McCard nodded. "You will have a concealed holster since you hopefully won't need to use it much. If they don't know you are armed they will save their guns for a last resort."

"Wouldn't it be better to show them I'm armed and let them waste their ammunition?"

"Not if you are dealing with a hostage situation. Once they discover the bullets don't hurt you, they will go for the people you are trying to save."

"That makes sense."

"Here's your new jacket, it should help you cover up your gun while you are out and about." McCard paused and Patrick could tell his dad was trying to sort out his words before he spoke. "There is one more thing we need to talk about."

Patrick placed the gun on the desk and followed his father back to the plush office chairs. Once they were seated, McCard began.

"Son, you were asking how a mask can make people not recognize you but the truth is, in reality, it won't always do that. There will be people smart enough to put two and two together and see through the flimsy mask."

"So, no matter how I disguise myself you and Mom will be in danger." Patrick summarized softly.

"Patrick, what you have to do can be done by no one else. The compound I stumbled across can never be reproduced as it was in you without the formula. You alone have 8/15 running through your veins making you indestructible. But, because you are human, you have loved and been loved. That is something that would hold you back, a weakness that would hinder you from using your true potential."

"So you are basically saying I would have to cut all ties and change my name?" Patrick asked seriously.

McCard sighed. "I don't see any other way. If you stayed

a McCard you would be constantly worrying about your mother and I."

Patrick nodded. "That's a big decision."

"I know. I wanted to give you time to think about it but there is not much time. There is an operation taking place in the city I will be sending you to. A ring of thieves are destroying the economics of the city, and the local law enforcement is helpless against them."

"I understand. What would my name be?"

"This is probably the worst day of your life isn't it? You lose your friend, your home, your name, and your family all in one day. I don't know how you can face it so bravely."

"I was born for this, Dad. Raised and trained for this. It is who I am, and who I must become."

McCard nodded, his eyes moist. "You are one of a kind Patrick, and I don't just mean the 8/15 either. As for the name, you can choose. You can have the name you designed if that is what you like. Or you can pick a different first name and keep only Roper. If you want to start from scratch there's a name book on the shelf."

"It's strange to be naming myself," Patrick said, uncomfortable with his father's tears.

"I'm so sorry to have to do this to you."

"Dad, you aren't doing anything to me. It's not the end, I can always come back."

McCard nodded. "Yes, once a year you will have the chance to return to normal life. If you look at a digital clock that shows the true time at exactly 8:15am on August 15th the compound will be neutralized and you will no longer be invincible."

"It's not forever. Just a season." Patrick told him quietly.

McCard nodded. "I can't tell you how much we will miss you."

"There is one thing…"

"What is it?"

"I didn't really get to say goodbye to Mom."

"She is flying in tomorrow for that purpose."

"Thanks for thinking of that." Patrick rose. He went to the shelf and pulled out the name book flipping aimlessly through the pages.

He was about to become someone he had prepared his entire life to be, but he was not sure he was ready.

Four

At 6:30 the following evening Jason Roper left M.C. Enterprises and walked down the crowded street. He wore black cargo pants and a black t-shirt. His left arm bumped comfortably against the Glock 23 concealed beneath his dark leather jacket. He stopped just outside the downtown bus station and shifted his well-used backpack on his shoulder. Looking back at the tall glass building, he let his breath out slowly. This was it. There was no turning back.

"Where to?" the man behind the counter asked roughly. He was a big man with matted hair and a crooked nose.

Jason leaned on the counter. "Can you tell me anything about the robberies going on in Centerville?"

"Centerville?" The man cocked his eyebrow at Jason. "Who fed you that?"

"I just heard there were some thieves…"

The big man laughed and slapped the counter. "You some kind of freelance hero? Listen, kid, Centerville is as quiet as a graveyard. I haven't heard a thing from that area in months, and I have connections."

Jason frowned. Why would his dad send him to Centerville if there was not really a problem?

"This guy thinks there's a ring of thieves in Centerville." The man told a rough looking man that was sitting a few feet from the counter.

The man grinned revealing a gold tooth and sauntered

over to them. "I bet he's another journalist looking for the scoop of his life." He clapped Jason on the back good-naturedly "Now, if you're looking for trouble, they've got their fair share in Franklin."

"What are you trying to do kill the boy?" the ticket man asked. "You're a nice looking guy, so I'll give you a hint. You don't wanna go to Franklin right now." His voice was ominous.

"What do you mean?" Jason asked innocently.

"It just ain't a pretty place nowadays. There's fightin' and killin'. Its just not a place for a nice city boy like yourself."

"Aw, come on. He wants a scoop doesn't he?" The gold tooth reappeared. "Listen, kid, there's the biggest racket in history out there. They've got the whole city wrapped around their little finger."

"What are they doing it for?" Jason was puzzled. There was a huge gang operating freely in Franklin but his dad was sending him in the opposite direction.

Both men laughed.

"They're doing it for money." He exchanged an amused look with the ticket man. "You are pretty fresh, aren't you? They're taking over all the major businesses. The ones who comply receive 'protection' and those who don't are shut down." He leaned in confidentially. "I've heard they are just a little side working of a much bigger ring."

"Get out of here, Markus. Your bus is here." The big man reached over the counter and shoved Markus away before turning back to Jason. "Don't pay him any mind. He likes to talk too much."

"It's the scoop of a life time." Markus laughed and strode out as the bus pulled to a stop.

"What can you tell me about the gang?" Jason asked seriously.

The big man eyed Jason, rubbing his crooked nose with his index finger. "Why are you so interested in this?"

Jason could tell he had used the wrong approach and quickly switched his tactics. "This is a great opportunity. I mean this could be my big break. If I can get this story I'll be in the big league." He paused and pretended to be unsure of himself. "They wouldn't bother a reporter, right?"

"Depends." The big man shrugged. "If you work with them they treat you alright, but I don't think I'd chance it."

"But I've got to go. This is the first break I've had in months. If I don't get this story I'll be living on the streets." Jason paused to fidget with the strap of his bag. "How much does the ticket cost?"

"Twenty bucks even. I can't refuse to sell it to you, but you ought to think this out more. These aren't like the little neighborhood gangs you are thinking of, these men mean business." He shrugged again. "Maybe there really are thefts in Centerville."

"If the racket is so big what do the normal people do?" Jason asked pulling out his wallet.

"There's not much they can do. The Jarris brothers have them tied hand and foot. Even the cops can't lift a finger to help.

"Have a lot of businesses given in?" Jason handed the man a twenty dollar bill.

"Yeah. Most gave in right off the bat." He put the twenty into his drawer and typed something into his computer before going on. "Last I heard there was only a few not shelling it out to Jarris and his boys." He slid Jason's ticket across the counter. "This station is not responsible if you lose your ticket, so keep an eye on it."

Jason nodded and slipped the ticket into his pocket. "I guess if I want to get a good story I'll have to get a place right in the middle of the city." Jason glanced around as if he did not trust the people milling about the station and then leaned across the counter. "Should I get me a gun or something?"

The big man shrugged. "That won't help much. The Jarris brothers use a range of artillery and are good at what they do. Just don't cross them."

"So what's my best bet for avoiding trouble?"

"Just stay out of their way, Anderson Street has been theirs from the start. I would steer clear of that area."

"How many brothers are there?"

"What difference does that make?" He eyed Jason suspiciously. "They got a dozen or so experienced men working for them."

"Just trying to get the facts." Jason replied with a shrug.

The big man was obviously losing interest so Jason dropped the subject, making sure he still appeared nervous about his upcoming trip. "How long will it take to get there?"

"Oh, about five hours I guess. Somewhere in that neighborhood."

"Okay." Jason licked his lips nervously. "I guess I'll wait over there."

The station man grinned at Jason's discomfort. "Lay low and you should be fine. I wouldn't sweat over it until you get there."

"Thanks." Jason went to a bench by the wall and sat down keeping his backpack on his lap. He considered giving his dad a call but decided against it. The ties were already legally cut, so he might as well get used to it. He sat back to watch the people come and go from the station. There were people everywhere, but Jason's eyes were attracted to a man wearing an old fedora, who walked through the bus station just about every twenty minutes as if checking for someone specific to arrive.

Five minutes before Jason's bus was scheduled to load, a nervous-looking man in his late twenties entered the station. Hurrying to the counter, he leaned far across it so as not to be overheard then quickly shelled out some well worn bills.

Taking his ticket, he shoved it deep into his pocket then turned to find a seat. Jason diverted his eyes as the man's eyes swept his end of the station. Jason's discretion was rewarded when the man came over and sat two seats away. Sweat poured down his face as he waited and he used an old handkerchief now and then to wipe it away. Shifting in his seat, his eyes never left the automatic doors.

The loudspeaker called out the bus number and destination causing Jason and the man to stand at the same time.

"Are you riding bus 34, too?" Jason asked.

The man spooked as if he had not noticed Jason sitting there. "Yeah, that's right I'm on bus 34." He was still looking around, his eyes darting here and there like a scared animal.

Jason took his time, fiddling with his backpack until the young man headed for the bus. Then he swung his backpack onto his shoulder and walked a little ways behind him.

The hunted man paused at the door then made a rush for the bus slamming into the man who stepped into his path. The man tipped his fedora politely but his look was deadly. "Evening, Edgar. Where you headed?"

The color drained from Edgar's face and he began to tremble.

"I don't remember anyone saying you could go anywhere."

"He's with me." Jason spoke gruffly. "I'm taking him to Anderson Street."

The man smiled cruelly. "So you're off to Anderson? I guess the Jarris brothers want to deal with you on their own."

Edgar stammered something Jason could not make out, but fear was clearly etched in his every feature.

"Get on up there." Jason's voice was anything but kind as he shoved Edgar toward the bus. "You know how they feel about people who keep them waiting."

FIVE

The bus had been rumbling along for close to an hour before Jason ventured to speak to his new companion.

"So, who was that guy?"

Edgar sat by the window where Jason had placed him. He was slouched in his seat and had not uttered a word since they had entered the bus.

"Edgar." Jason touched his arm and Edgar started as if he had been burned. "Listen, I'm not going to hurt you. I don't work for the Jarris brothers."

Edgar shoved Jason's hand away.

"I'm not taking you to them. I said it so that guy wouldn't carry you off. Are you listening at all?"

Edgar braced himself as the bus lurched over a rut in the road. "Yeah, thanks for nothin'." He mumbled.

"Edgar, look at me."

He did. The look of fear and hurt in his eyes swallowed up the fierceness he attempted to show. Jason fell silent, he had never seen such a haunted look.

"You've been through it, haven't you?" Jason finally managed when Edgar looked away.

"What's it to you?" Edgar asked still trying to sound tough.

"Nothing I guess. I just didn't want to see you get pounded."

"So, you are taking me right to them."

"Hey, you are the one who bought the ticket. I just helped you get on. Why are you on this bus anyway?"

"I had to get out and it was the only chance I had." Edgar was finally starting to relax a little. "What about you? You don't seem the type to be going to Anderson Street."

"I've got a job there." Jason told him bluntly.

"Then you are working for them." Edgar turned to look out the dirty window. "Figures."

"No, I'm not." Jason stretched his arms up to touch the roof of the bus. "This seat was not designed for long rides."

"What are you doing there if you aren't working for the brothers?" Edgar pressed.

"I got a job." Jason didn't know what his job would be, his dad had always told him his mission was to stop crime and save the innocent, but now that he was on his own he was not sure how to go about it.

"What kind of job?" Edgar's eyes were probing.

"What does it matter what kind it is?" Jason asked, truly irritated. "That's my business."

"I can take a hint." Edgar slouched in his seat and returned his gaze to the scenery outside. The bus moved over the rough road and both men soon drifted off to sleep.

———

"Hey." Someone roughly bumped Jason's shoulder and he started from a sound sleep. "This is the last stop. You'd better get off with the rest of them."

Jason looked beside him, the seat was empty. The last few passengers were filing slowly out of the bus into the dark streets but Edgar was not among them. Instinctively Jason checked his pocket. The fifty his dad had given him to get started was gone.

"The rat." Jason muttered. He rose and swung his backpack onto his back as he hurried down the aisle of the bus, pausing on the top step to survey the area. In the dim glow of a streetlight Jason made out Edgar's thin form as he slipped out of view into a dark alley.

"Excuse me." Jason pushed his way through the people milling at the station and sprinted to the alley where Edgar had disappeared. He arrived in time to see Edgar round the next corner. Jason moved quickly, dodging the piles of trash that cluttered the alley. Edgar did not know he was being followed so Jason still had the upper hand. They had rounded a few more corners, Jason silently closing the gap between them, when his foot snagged on an old beer bottle. It fell with a clatter rolling loudly across the pavement.

Edgar looked back, and then broke into a run. Jason followed, the backpack bouncing uncomfortably on his back as he ran. He cinched up the straps to lessen its bucking and ran smack into a wide man who had been standing out of sight around the corner Edgar had just taken.

"Sorry." Jason tried to go around him but the man grabbed the front of his shirt and pulled him down to his level.

"Listen, I've already been robbed by that jerk." Jason told him pointing down the alley.

The big man turned to look at Edgar who had paused at the end of the alley to watch the show. "Well, this is my territory, I charge an entrance fee."

His breath reeked of beer and sausage causing Jason's stomach to churn. He moved his head back to get out of breathing range. "If you want money you have to take it from him because he already took it from me."

"I'll deal with him later, but I think you got more." The man responded, flipping open a jackknife uncomfortably close to Jason's stomach.

Jason hesitated, curious to see the effect of a knife on his now invincible body. Would it penetrate without pain or simply strike the surface as if he were made of steel?

"Well?" his attacker shook him roughly.

Jason saw Edgar was slowly edging his way out of the alley.

The big man did not see Jason's fist, it connected squarely with his jaw and he reeled back from the impact. Dodging around him, Jason raced after Edgar once more.

There was twenty feet between them and Jason could see the young man was beginning to tire. "Edgar, all I want is my money. Give it to me and I'll leave you alone." Jason called. Edgar did not answer. He stumbled on a trash pile but caught himself and ran on.

"You ungrateful rat, I saved your life." There was only ten feet between them now and Edgar picked up speed. He was obviously headed somewhere close. Jason moved forward with a burst of speed, closing the gap between them once more. Up ahead a door opened and Edgar dove in. Someone pulled it shut from the inside but Jason's arm was already in the door. The thought occurred to him that having the door slammed on his arm would usually have hurt, but he dismissed it as he fought to pry the door open.

"Edgar, I'm not going until I have it," Jason yelled, forcing the door open a little wider.

A gun appeared in the gap Jason had made and Jason could see right down the barrel. He grabbed the gun. Knocking the barrel upward and apparently catching whoever was holding it off guard. The gun went off shattering a window high above them. Jason wrenched the gun out of the man's hand and turned it on him.

"Open this door or I'll start shooting," Jason threatened.

There was some discussion then the door was freed. It swung open with a bang and Jason found himself facing a room full of men, all heavily armed.

Jason hesitated for a moment seeing how helpless his odds were and then cleared his throat. "I'm here for my money." He informed them lowering the gun to his side.

"What money is that?" The speaker was an older man with an evil glint in his eye. His graying hair was combed and his clothes were neat, but his eyes showed the wicked-ness of his heart.

"I presume you are Mr. Jarris." Jason observed toying with the gun he held.

"And what if I am?" Mr. Jarris' thin face showed no sign of ever having been creased with a smile.

Jason shrugged off the question. "I'm here for the money Edgar stole from me on the bus."

"The bus station is nearly two miles away." The man behind Jarris observed. His hair was fiery red and a long scar marred his face. He turned to Edgar. "Did he trail you all that way?"

Edgar, still out of breath only nodded. Jason saw the fear had returned to his eyes.

"I came to start fresh. I've got a job here and I don't plan on starting without that money." Jason told them boldly.

"What sort of job are you starting?" Jarris asked casually.

"You won't get anything from me until I get my money." Jason stated bluntly.

"You got a lot of nerve." The scarred man moved forward to strike him, but Jarris called him back.

"There will be time for that later, Frank. Edgar, give him his cash."

Edgar dug in his pocket and pulled out the fifty and handed it begrudgingly to Jason.

"Thanks." Jason shoved the bill into his own pocket and tossed the gun to Frank who caught it gingerly.

"Now, let's talk." Jarris motioned toward an empty chair.

Jason took the chair and moved it closer to the door before sitting down. "What can I do for you?"

"That's what I would like to know." Jarris smiled. "You see, I have several open positions for a man like you."

"You don't know anything about me." Jason told him.

"Ah, but I do. You trailed Edgar two miles for fifty dollars. You have persistence and stamina. That's what I need."

Jason waited for Jarris to go on.

"I have a new part of town I am…remodeling and there are a few people I'd like to move out of the way. If you take the job it will be on a test basis, you will contact Frank here for your orders."

"So I will have no contact with any of you higher ups so that if I squeal, nobody can prove anything." Jason observed without emotion.

"You catch on quick." Jarris was obviously pleased.

"Alright, I'll give it a try."

"What's your name?"

"Roper." Jason answered without hesitation.

"Just Roper huh? No first name?"

"I'd rather go by Roper for now."

"Alright Roper, we will humor you for the moment. Keep in mind we are a close-working team. Any sign of betrayal will be severely punished. Do I make myself clear?"

"Very." Jason rose.

"Good, Frank will show you your room." Jarris turned to Frank. "Put him in the empty room at Mary's place. I think we could use a little more supervision there."

Frank nodded. "That's a good idea. Come along Mr. Roper, I'll show you to your quarters."

———

Jason followed Frank through the dark streets. They passed well lighted casinos and several dim bars but the respectable people were safe in their beds behind locked doors. Frank stopped in front of a big two-story house.

"This is Mary's place."

"Does she work for Jarris?" Jason was imagining the bar girl type of woman.

Frank chuckled, "I guess you could put it that way."

"How would you put it?" Jason asked looking up at the beautiful house. Even in the dim glow of the street light Jason could tell it was kept up fairly well.

"She's the only one living in this big old house. She didn't need that much space and Jarris had a couple of guys who needed a place to stay."

"How much does she charge?"

Frank banged loudly on the door. "She doesn't charge, Jarris lets her stay, so she lets his men stay." Frank banged again and an older woman opened the door slightly. "What do you want?"

Frank shoved open the door. "I've got another boarder for you, Mary. Make sure he's comfortable."

"I don't have a room," Mary protested weakly.

"I said make him comfortable." Frank's voice was threatening and Mary fell silent. "Kernigan ain't living here anymore, put Roper here in his old room."

"I haven't had a chance to clean it," Mary told him, her voice held a twinge of fear. She was a thin, worn out woman. Her plain dress was mostly hidden by a shabby housecoat that had long ago faded to a drab brown. Her white hair was pulled up into a loose bun but wispy strands hung down around her tired face.

"She'll show you to your room." Frank informed Jason before striding off down the street.

She watched Frank go, then sighed. "This way." She trudged up the staircase and pushed open the first door she came to.

"How much is the room," Jason asked.

"There's no charge," she told him dully before turning to leave.

"How much do you charge the other renters?"

She paused on the step as if debating her answer then continued her slow descent. "There'll be no charge."

"I've only got a fifty," Jason told her following her down.

She turned to look up at him, clearly puzzled. "Are you trying to make trouble for me?"

"No, Ma'am." Jason understood that Jarris' men usually didn't pay, but he hadn't thought about it hurting her. "I brought the fifty for my room the first nights. I don't know when I'll get my first pay but this can cover the first week and once I start getting paid I can give you the rest. I know it's not much…"

"It's more than I've gotten from any of the others," Mary muttered bitterly.

"You'll take it then?" Jason asked, digging in his pocket for the bill.

She sighed and nodded. He gave the fifty to her and she started back down the steps just as the front door opened. Mary shoved the money into the pocket of her housecoat but not before the newcomer spotted it.

"What you got there Mary? Somethin' for me?" He reached for the bill.

"Leave her alone." Jason's tone was firm.

"Yeah? And who's gonna make me?" The man was about three inches shorter than Jason. He tilted his head to get a better look at Jason who was coming down the stairs. Jason noted his bloodshot eyes and had a pretty good idea where this man had been. His clothes were rumpled and his once blond hair was dirty and matted with grease.

"I'll make you if that's what you want," Jason answered. "I paid her for my room, not you."

"Who do you think you are?" He moved closer and Jason caught a glimpse of the gun that was shoved under his belt.

"I work for Jarris." Jason smiled at the man's expression. "Didn't know you were crossing him did you?"

"How do I know you aren't just makin' it up?"

"Ask Frank, he's the one who brought me here."

He turned on Mary. "Is that true?"

She nodded fearfully.

"Alright, so she can keep it."

"The name's Roper." Jason held out his hand.

"Murphy." He replied ignoring Jason's hand.

"I guess you'll be the one showing me the ropes around here."

Murphy shrugged. "Not likely, I don't do babysitting, not even for Jarris."

Without another word he climbed the stairs and disappeared into the room across from Jason's.

———

Jason set his backpack on the dresser and flopped down on the bed. The digital clock read 2:25am. Almost without thinking, Jason dragged himself to his feet and turned the clock to the wall. He lay down once more with a sigh. This was not exactly what he had had in mind. When he had left M.C. Enterprises he thought he would be tangling with a little petty theft, but here he was trying to single-handedly clear up a major gang that had already taken over most of the city. Jason smiled in the darkness. It had been a crazy night. Not only had he met the man he was trying to capture, but he was now an employee of the big man himself. He ran his fingers through his dirty hair and sighed again. Tomorrow he would be playing a tough man, trying to worm his way deeper into the workings of the enemy.

Six

A heavy knock roused Jason from his sleep. He rolled to a sitting position and blinked wearily at the visitor.

"So you don't carry a weapon?" Frank asked. He pulled out the desk chair and sat straddling it.

"What?" Jason felt stiff but there was no pain. He rubbed his eyes and looked at Frank again. "What are you talking about?"

"You didn't go for it. A man who is used to carrying a weapon always goes for it when he is startled out of sleep."

"Oh. So I pass the test?"

Frank laughed. "I guess so. Murphy told me about you paying Mary for your room." Frank's voice did not reveal how he felt about what Jason had done.

Jason shrugged and got up. "I figure it's only fair."

"You'll get over that soon enough." Frank told him.

Jason ran his hands through his hair. "Do showers come with the boarding deal? I feel like I haven't had one in a week."

Frank smiled and the look he gave Jason made him very uncomfortable. "Anything you want comes with the deal. You want it you take it. That's the way it is when you are working for Jarris."

Jason tried to look impressed. "Looks like I'm on the right side of things."

Frank rose to go. "I'll meet you outside in thirty minutes."

Jason nodded. "I'll be there."

———

"Hello Jason, sit down."

"I believe I made it clear that I prefer Roper," Jason answered stiffly. He stood in the same doorway as he had the night before which he now knew was the back entrance of a junky convenience store.

Frank smiled, obviously amused. "Silas here did a little research on you last night."

"So?" Jason folded his arms on his chest and leaned against the doorframe. Silas' hair was somewhere between brown and blond. Jason guessed him to be in his late thirties. His build and height were average, and there was nothing about his features that would have made him stand out in a crowd.

"Will you be seated?" Silas asked, with a forced politeness.

"I haven't been asked." Jason met the man's eyes without flinching. He saw Frank shift uncomfortably behind him but Silas was not fazed by Jason's boldness.

"You're that opposed to your name?" Silas asked leaning back in his chair.

"I believe there are some things I have a right to choose."

Silas nodded. "There are a few." He thought for a moment then shrugged. "I have no problem with you going by Roper if that's what you prefer."

"It is." Jason took the offered chair and sat facing the men.

Frank took a chair in the far corner and took out a pack of cigarettes.

"Do that outside, Frank." Silas told him coolly. Frank rose and trudged out of the makeshift office.

"Alright, Roper. How would you like to hear a little history?"

"I've got nothing to hide," Jason replied tilting his chair back against the wall.

"You were born Jason H. Roper on April 30th..." Silas scanned the papers before him. "What does the H stand for?"

"Beats me," Jason lied with a shrug. "I guess they just made something up to fill the blank." He knew what it stood for. The H was for "Hues" to remind Jason of his original "superhero name". It was like a little gift from his father to remind him of his former life.

By the way the older man looked at him, he knew it was a lie, but Silas did not press the issue.

"Your parents died in a car accident just after your 18th birthday and now you are making your way in the big world."

"I guess you could put it that way." Jason answered carelessly. "I've been on my own for a while now."

"I see you kept a pretty clean record for yourself." Silas observed without looking up from the page. "No arrests to speak of."

"To speak of?" Jason asked. "I think no arrests period would be more accurate."

Silas nodded. "Looks good for us, and you."

"So, when do I meet Mr. Jarris' brother?" Jason was rewarded by a surprised then threatening look.

"You will deal directly with Frank. Only in select emergencies will you have contact with me or anyone else above him," Silas told him firmly.

"So, the Mr. Jarris I met is the lower contact and the brother is the high untouchable?"

"I'd leave that subject alone, Roper." There was a threatening twinge in the man's voice and Jason complied. He had learned what he wanted to know and would take the time to research it better later on.

"Okay, what are my orders?"

"There is a storeowner on Roger Ave. who needs to be out by next week."

"Pretty short notice," Jason observed.

"He's had his fair share of warnings. I'll send Gary with you to show you how it's done."

Jason nodded thoughtfully. "So I'm just tagging along for this one?"

"You could put it that way." Silas stood and opened the door to his right. Through it Jason could see the well stocked shelves and dirty floor of the convenience store.

"Gary, you have a second?" Silas called.

"Sure, be right there."

A big man with a grizzly face appeared a moment later. "Yeah?"

"This is Roper, he'll be going to Taylor's with you this afternoon."

Gary looked at Jason and grinned. "A little wet behind the ears, isn't he?"

"He'll do fine, Jarris said he's the one for the job."

"If Jarris likes him, I guess he'll have to do." He pointed a thick finger at Jason. "Meet me here at eleven sharp."

Jason nodded once to show he had heard and Gary disappeared back into the store.

"I guess you see why Jarris chose Gary to do the final warning." Silas looked amused.

"Not really." Jason answered, rising and pushing his chair back to where it had been.

"You seemed pretty subdued," Silas observed.

Jason shrugged. "Take it how you like. If I look wet behind the ears to him it gives me the upper hand."

"How so?"

"Anything I do will catch him off guard."

"Hmm." Silas looked thoughtful. "I see where you are coming from."

"Am I free to go?" Jason asked.

"Yes, just be back at eleven, which gives you about an hour to get a feel of the city."

SEVEN

Jason wandered aimlessly through the streets, pausing now and then to observe the local architecture. The weathered historic signs and unkempt flowerbeds reminded the residents of what their town had once been. Up ahead he saw a big sign that said "Taylor's" in red and blue lettering. Jason meandered over to the store and through the glass door. The air was chilly inside and Jason was grateful for his jacket. The checkout stands were neatly lined up to his right and the store was alive with the morning shoppers. Taylor's showed no sign of shutting down.

"Can I help you, sir?" a smiling man in a suit asked coming toward him.

"No," Jason shoved his hands into his pockets. "I was just looking."

"Feel free to browse, any of my employees will be more than glad to help you if you can't find what you are looking for." Jason noticed the man's eyes were tired.

"Thanks." Jason drifted further in and waited until he had gone, before leaving the store. This afternoon's meeting would be interesting.

Jason walked a little longer on the street to be sure he was not being followed then cut down a side street. He had thirty minutes to find the police department and be back to meet with Gary at the office. It would be tight but Jason knew he needed to connect with the police before he got too involved with the gang. He needed a contact, someone he could tip off and deliver his information to. The only problem was he could not ask. He had no idea who was on Jarris' payroll and who was simply suffering under his rule. He passed several people on the street but all seemed to be in a hurry to get somewhere and most wouldn't even meet his eyes. He looked at his watch, twenty minutes left and there was no sign of the station or any police for that matter.

He was about to give up when he spotted a man in uniform up ahead.

Jason walked swiftly to catch up with him while at the same time trying not to attract the attention of the people on the street. "Excuse me, sir."

The officer stopped, and gave Jason a wary look. "What is it?"

Jason was disappointed. The officer was young and obviously a rookie.

"I was just wondering…" He paused. He had suspected the common people of being involved with Jarris but it suddenly struck him that the police could also be on Jarris' side. If the police were working for the big man, it made sense that they would not have stopped the rising tide of crime in the area.

"Well, get on with it," the officer told him.

"I am a reporter from out of town." Jason lied. "I was wondering if you could tell me about this new gang outbreak in your area."

"Outbreak? I think you mean takeover, and it is not new."

Jason could tell he had hit the jackpot. "What do you mean?"

"They call it the Jarris brothers' gang but no one has heard anything about any brother. Very few have seen Jarris, that's what we call the leader, but as for a brother, there's no proof that he even exists. I guess he could be some big wig who is directing things from another area."

"Have your men been able to put up a pretty good resistance?" Jason asked. He wished he had brought along a little notepad or something to make himself look more professional but the rookie officer did not seem to care about credibility.

"Are you kidding me? We are tied hand and foot. We can't lift our little finger against them without being slapped down. They know about all our raids, all our stakeouts, it's as if all our activities were being broadcast to the whole network of gangsters."

"So you suspect foul play?" Jason probed.

"You mean like a spy? We followed that lead months ago and came up empty handed…"

Jason noticed someone loitering in the shadows about a block down who was obviously watching him. He let the officer prattle on for a while nodding enough to keep him going. Then cut in.

"This has been very informative. I would like to meet with you another time if that would be possible."

"Oh," the officer was obviously flattered. "I have most Tuesdays off."

"Great, Tuesdays are perfect." Jason found the bus ticket in his pocket and pulled it out. "Can I get your name and the name of the chief or whoever is in charge of this station."

"Sure, I'm officer Bert Bently." He patted his pockets and came up with a pen. "Here, that's B-e-n-t-l-y."

"And the guy in charge?" Jason's time was almost gone. He scribbled down "Bently" to make the officer happy then waited with his pen poised over the paper. Out of the corner of his eye Jason saw the man in the shadows was coming toward him.

"That would be Bill Lario," Bert told him. "William really, but he goes by Bill."

"Thanks, Mr. Bently." Jason shoved the bus ticket into his pocket.

"Call me Bert, it was no problem at all."

"Great, thanks." Jason was backing away, trying to leave without being overly rude.

Once he was around the corner Jason broke into a steady jog. If he was careful he could still make it on time without arriving out of breath.

"Hey!"

Jason groaned inside. So his shadow had not left him. He turned and jogged backwards.

"Dude, I have an appointment, you'll have to take a number," Jason turned back around and jogged on. Glancing back, Jason noticed that his pursuer was not much older than himself, and was keeping up quite well.

"Stop!" The guy was closing in.

"Listen, I can meet with you later," Jason called over his shoulder.

Jason had just reached a nice straight stretch when a lady screamed, "He's got a gun!" as if she were practicing for a Hollywood job as an actress. The street cleared rapidly and Jason slowed for the sake of the public. He was rewarded with the distinct feeling of a gun barrel in his back.

"What do you want?" Jason demanded without turning around.

"I'll ask the questions," he replied pushing harder with the gun. "Why were you talking with that cop?"

"Because he was talking to me," Jason responded. "Go easy with the gun man. I'm not doing anything."

Jason felt him relax a little. "What were you writing down?"

Jason gave a short laugh. "His name, the guy was all ego. The paper is in my pocket."

He reached for it, but Jason moved away. "I can get it." He faced the gun as he pulled the bus ticket out and showed his pursuer the back. The word Bently was scrawled across the paper. "Happy?"

He looked Jason over while Jason gave him the same treatment. Jason guessed him to be was around nineteen. He was an inch or two taller than Jason and his brown hair and eyes, were a shade lighter.

"Listen, I have to get to this little store place in three minutes, do you mind if we at least walk while you hold me up?"

"This isn't a hold up, you dope." He responded shoving the gun back into its holster. "I just had to make you stop." He fell in beside Jason. "I don't think your story will hold much water with the higher ups."

"Meaning?"

"You're probably in for some interrogation tonight."

"So you work for Jarris, too?" Jason asked.

"Too?"

"Yeah, I'm meeting one of his men at eleven, which is now." Jason answered looking at his watch. "It's my first assignment and I'm not making a very good impression, thanks to you. What's your name so I can blame it on you?"

"Benjamin, Benjamin Curr." He replied with a hint of pride. "And don't even try to blame it on me. You talking with a copper will knock anything you say about me. I'll see you around."

"Sure, make me late and then let me face them alone." Jason was not impressed.

Benjamin laughed, "Happy shopping." He obviously knew about the visit to Taylor's, Jason wondered how long this had been planned.

Jason rounded the last corner exactly five minutes after eleven. Gary was standing outside the store with his big fists planted firmly on his hips, looking like a grizzly robbed of her cubs.

"Don't bother with any excuses." Gary told him, his brow furrowed ominously. "I'll deal with you later."

"Yes, Sir." Jason answered meekly. He had heard that

a soft answer would turn away anger. This was the perfect time to try it out.

"Let's go." Gary climbed into the dark sedan that was parked on the curb and put it in gear. Jason just managed to jump in before the car lurched forward. Gary switched the air on and Jason was enveloped in the stale factory smell of the new car. They rode in silence as Gary guided the car through the streets, ten minutes passed before they pulled into the parking lot. Gary stopped the car right in front of the doors of Taylor's, smack in the middle of the crosswalk. No one objected, the people leaving the store simply walked around it. Gary got out and walked purposely into the store with Jason tagging along like a shamed puppy.

The door to the manager's office banged against the wall as Gary walked through. Jason caught it before it could slam shut and quietly closed it. The man behind the desk jumped to his feet. It was the cheerful man with the tie who had offered to help Jason on his previous visit. The manager apparently recognized Jason as well.

"What do you want?" His cheerful smile had been replaced by a thin determined line.

"I think you know." Gary's voice carried a threat.

"Well, you go tell Jarris that I'm not accepting his so-called protection and I'm not clearing out. This is my place. Permanently." The last word was emphasized by the appearance of a well polished hand gun that was aimed at Gary's wide chest. "Get out."

"You'll be sorry, Taylor." Gary told him.

Jason watched as Gary left the room.

"You too." The gun swung around toward Jason who had gotten so caught up in the drama that he forgot what side he was on.

"Yes, Sir." Scurrying for the door, he slipped out and shut it behind himself. He hurried after Gary but when he got outside the car was already pulling away.

Jason hesitated, unsure of what he was expected to do. He checked the street before reentering the store. Pushing open the manager's door, Jason was met once more with the barrel of the gun.

"I thought I made it clear…"

"You did." Jason interrupted. He entered the office and shut the door behind him. "I don't know how to say this."

"I do. Get out of my store before I add an extra button hole to your jacket." The manager was plain mad.

"That was a very good way to put it." Jason told him putting up his hands in an effort to calm the man. "I am not here to…"

"I didn't ask why you were here," the manager cut in, "and frankly I don't care."

Jason checked the area outside the door. No one was around. "Okay, I can see I am trying to be too nice. The truth is I am here to help you. Make sense? I'm just playing along to keep them off guard."

"And you expect me to believe that?"

"No, not really. But I want you to know it so when the time comes you'll be ready." Jason shoved his hands in his pockets but the look Taylor gave him made him pull them back out again. "The only catch is you are the only one who knows I am here to help. This is my first official day here and I haven't had time to set up any contacts."

The manager was still wary but he was listening, so Jason went on. "I don't know how to tell who is part of the gang and who is not so I don't know who to set up in my network of contacts. The reason I am telling you is that you are the first person who is definitely not a part of the gang."

The manager sharply let out his breath, disgusted. "You could tell, could you?"

"If we are going to get rid of these overlords we…"

"There's no we, I don't know who you are, but I know who you were with, and I'm not doing any business with you. End of meeting." He gestured to the door with his gun and Jason had no choice but to obey.

Not knowing what to do next, Jason returned to Mary's house where he knew they would be able to find him when he was needed. The door was unlocked and he went straight up to his room. He paused with his hand on the doorknob. Something wasn't right. A cold fear surged through him and he let go of the knob. He was tempted to run, as fast and as far as he could but something held him back. He turned the knob and shoved the door open taking a step back as he did. There, lounging on his bed was Frank. Silas was leaning against the dresser with a 45 dangling lazily from his hand.

"What is this?" Jason asked looking from one to the other.

"What took you so long?" Silas asked rubbing an invisible spot on the barrel of the gun.

"Gary left me at the store. I didn't know if I was supposed to wait or not so I hung around the store a bit. When he didn't show I came here."

"That so?" Frank asked sitting up. "What were you doing while you were 'hanging around'?"

"I just looked around the store." Jason was becoming a fluent liar. "It was uncomfortable though with the manager breathing down my neck the whole time so, like I said, I came here."

"What about the cop you were fraternizing with earlier?" Frank pressed.

"Benjamin certainly doesn't waste time." Jason observed. "It was his fault I got to the store late. He had to pull the 'obey me, I have a gun' stunt and what else could I do?"

"Benjamin does his job, and he does it well," Silas told him. "You would do well to follow his example."

"I've only been here one day," Jason argued. "I don't see

how I'm supposed to learn everything in one day."

"Jarris doesn't like excuses. You'll learn fast or you'll find yourself on the other end."

Jason glared at the floor and did not answer him.

"So, what were you discussing with the cop?" Frank asked again.

"Lay off, Frank." Jason told him harshly. He turned to Silas. "I told you before, I got nothing to hide. I wanted to see how the cops viewed the gang, kind of get a feel for the opposition. I asked him about it and he told me. I told him I was a reporter and he told me everything he knew."

"And what was that?" Silas' tone had lost its edge, and Jason relaxed a little.

"He said 'the gang' hears about everything they plan before they do it and that they are quote: 'tied hand and foot.'" Jason shrugged. "That's it."

"Nothing else?"

"Not unless you count the whole here's my name and these are my days off. The guy was full of himself."

Silas nodded. "Alright. You understand that we have to be careful with our new recruits, it's nothing against you, we're just playing it safe."

"That's it?" Frank asked incredulously.

Silas turned on him. "I said we are done."

"Jarris likes us to be a bit more…"

"He's fine Frank. Leave it."

Jason watched them as they stood facing one another, tense and ready for a fight. He wondered if all the relation-ships within the gang were held together with the same tense distrust mixed with fearful respect. Frank was the first to give in. He shouldered past Jason and disappeared down the steps. A moment later the front door slammed shut.

"Get some rest, you're going to need it." Silas told Jason as he started down the stairs.

"Where do I go next?" Jason asked.

"Frank will contact you."

"So I'm stuck here?" Jason wasn't happy with that option and Silas read it in his voice.

"He'll come tonight around ten." Silas paused before adding. "You'd better get used to it. You live on Jarris' schedule now."

Eight

Jason sat up, still groggy from sleep. He looked around the little room wondering what had awakened him. A light scratching from the door drew his attention and he pushed back the covers and slid out of bed. Standing against the wall he reached across and opened the door. A little tabby pushed it open more as she slid through. She looked up at Jason, acknowledging his presence, before strolling across the carpet and hopping gracefully onto the bed. She sat there watching him intently. Jason had never had a pet of his own and he wasn't sure what he was supposed to do with the little visitor. He flipped on the light and moved closer to the cat. It had no collar. Jason shooed it off the bed and straightened the covers. When he turned around the tabby was lying contentedly on the desk, still watching him.

"Listen," Jason told the cat, "I'm really not a cat person, not any animal really." He checked his Glock, grateful he had not had to use it. He wondered why Jarris' men hadn't bothered to frisk him. Perhaps they already knew he had it and were just biding their time. He opened his backpack and checked the contents. This too was becoming a habit. Everything was just as he had left it. Jason glanced at his watch. He still had four hours to kill. He left the room pulling the door closed behind him. He was halfway down the stairs when the cat meowed. Jason groaned and retraced his steps. Opening the door he watched as the cat squeezed out and scurried to the ground floor. Down below Jason heard the front door open. He paused to listen and he heard the refrigerator open. It was Murphy. He usually went straight to the fridge to see what Mary had gotten at the store that day. Jason hurried out closing the door softly behind him. He didn't have time to waste on Murphy. He took his time strolling through the neighborhood, making sure he was not being followed, then made a beeline for the police department.

The officer at the desk looked up as he entered and kept looking.

"I'm here to see Mr. Lario." Jason told him.

"What do you want with him?" he was an older officer, experienced and hardened.

"I have a message for him," Jason replied.

"You can leave your message with me and I'll pass it on."

Jason stood undecided for a moment as the officer came around the desk.

"You and the rest of those worthless gangsters can go right back where you came from," he told Jason bitterly, coming uncomfortably close.

Jason backed off. This man had obviously been hurt recently by the Jarris gang, but Jason didn't have time for sympathy. "Will Taylor be free around ten?"

The officer folded his arms across his chest. "Listen, buddy, you may feel all cool and sleek with your black garb and gangster connections, but you won't make it far with this gig."

"I don't intend to," Jason told him.

A drunk stumbled through the door escorted by another officer. The officer released the drunk, allowing him to slump onto the bench by the wall.

"Wayne, would you keep and eye on him while I get the paperwork?"

"Sure, Joe." The officer turned back to Jason.

"You can't tell me what to do." Jason told him belligerently. The drunk's act was a little too good and Jason could not afford to chance it. "You had no right dragging me in here just because you think I look like a gangster. It isn't a crime to wear black."

"You can wear whatever you want. Just keep out of trouble or you'll be seeing the inside of this place again."

"Yeah, right." Jason said over his shoulder as he stormed out.

"What was that about?" Joe asked putting the paper work on the desk.

"Some punk trying to be tough." Wayne told him. "What do you have?"

"Just another drunk." Joe shrugged. "It seems like that is all we get now a days, while the real threat evades us."

"I wish we could pin down the leaders," Wayne agreed pulling the drunk to his feet. "Come on, buddy, a day or two in the slammer ought to help you sober up."

"There was something strange about that boy," Wayne told Joe when he returned from locking up the drunk.

"What's that?" Joe asked scanning the paperwork.

"He knew the chief's name but then he asked if Taylor would be free."

Joe glanced up. "That is strange."

"There isn't a Taylor here," Wayne reminded him. "I don't think we've ever had an officer by that name."

Joe tapped the end of his pen on the papers for a moment. "Do you think he meant Taylor as in the Taylor's store?"

"That's a thought. If I remember right he asked if Taylor would be free at ten."

Joe's eyes met Wayne's. "They're hitting Taylor's tonight."

"It's a long shot but it's the only lead we've had in months." Wayne was excited.

"What do you say we do this one on our own?" Joe asked tentatively. "We are both off duty tonight, what if you and I just drive out there."

Wayne looked skeptical.

"Wayne, every time we tell the chief, we can't get through. He either brushes it off as a fake tip, or someone blows our cover and we lose the chance."

Wayne hesitated, not wanting to admit it.

"So, what do you say?"

Wayne looked at Joe for a moment then nodded slowly. "I owe it to Clive."

"Alright, I'll pick you up at 9:30."

Wayne shook his head. "I hope we are doing the right thing."

————

Jason stood outside the diner, his stomach growling like a hungry tiger. His mouth watered as he looked at the pictures of tempting dishes on the large windows.

"This is lame," Jason told himself turning away. He shoved his hands into his empty pockets and walked slowly away, the smell of freshly cooked burgers lingering in the wind. He returned to Mary's and sat forlornly on the front steps. This whole hero business was not bringing in much cash.

He watched the people hurrying home to their hot dinners, imagining what each was having. He felt something rubbing against him and looked down. It was the tabby.

"Shoo," Jason told it lifting his hand out of the way. The cat rubbed against his leg purring loudly. "I don't have any food if that's what you want." Jason told her pushing her away. She returned, purring even louder.

"Seems she's taken a liking to you," Mary observed.

Jason stood quickly. "I'm not much of an animal person."

Mary shifted her grocery sack on her hip and smiled. "That little cat doesn't seem to agree."

"Is it yours?" Jason asked.

"No. She took a liking to Mr. Kernigan when he was living here. But I hadn't seen her since his death."

"What happened to him?"

"Oh, there was a shootout of some sort over on Anderson. That's where a lot of the things like that happen. They say Kernigan shot an officer, I believe his name was Cliff or Clive or something like that. Anyway, I don't know if I believe it. Kernigan was not like the others, there was a kindness in him still." She paused, shifting her sack again. "He was a lot like you."

Jason looked at the cat who was still rubbing against his legs, leaving little gray and tan hairs on his black cargo pants. "So he killed whoever it was and a copper shot him?" He gently pushed the cat away with his foot, but she came back like a magnet, coating his other leg with tiny hairs.

"That's the story they tell around here." Mary shrugged, "There's no telling what really happened." She started up the steps and Jason pushed the door open for her. "Have you eaten lately?" she asked pausing in the doorway. "Murphy just eats whenever he wants to so I don't really think about feeding anyone."

"I haven't gotten paid yet," Jason told her quietly.

"That doesn't matter. What you gave me is enough to know you're an honest man. You can pay the rest when you get it."

Jason nodded, too hungry to resist. "I guess I could use a little something."

"I guess you could, you look like one of those active boys, the kind that need a lot of feeding."

Jason smiled, carefully shutting the cat out before following her into the kitchen. "Don't bother making anything. I can just eat whatever you have left over."

"Murphy makes sure there are never any leftovers here." There was a little irritation in her voice. "I'll whip something up for you. It will only take a minute."

"Can I help with anything?" Jason asked.

"Nope, just sit down there and let me work," Mary told him setting the sack down on the counter. She cleared the dirty dishes Murphy had left and opened the refrigerator to survey the damage.

"Seems like I have to go shopping every day now," she complained, more to herself than to Jason.

"What would happen if you just didn't?"

She looked at Jason as if he were crazy. "They'd take my house, and I'd be out on the street with no place to go. As long as I'm useful they let me stay."

Jason sat watching her as she worked, wondering how he could help her get out from under Jarris' thumb. If only he could find the brother. The man at the bus station had clearly said the Jarris Brothers, but as far as Jason could tell the other brother was off limits.

Jason looked up at the wall clock, it was eight-thirty. He had not been able to figure out what exactly he was going to do to stop the raid on Taylor's. Jason wondered if the officer had understood his tip.

"You sure are far away," Mary observed setting a plate of food in front of Jason.

"I'm sorry, I have a lot on my mind."

"If you don't mind me asking, how is it a nice boy like yourself got mixed up with someone like Frank?"

"He offered a job when I needed one," Jason answered.

"Doesn't the stealing and killing bother you?" Mary asked handing him a glass of water.

Jason took a swig of water, a shadow on the wall caught his eye. It was the unmistakable shape of the head and shoulders of a man. Probably Murphy. Jason set the glass down on the table.

"Not really. This isn't the first thing like this I have been involved in." He took a bite of his sandwich. "You get used to it after awhile. It's really just another way of making a living."

"By stealing from those who work hard for what they have?" Mary asked bitterly.

Jason shrugged. "Jarris hired me, so I do what he says. It's as simple as that."

"Don't you have any morals of your own?"

Again Jason shrugged. "I guess not," he said around his sandwich. He saw the shadow move slowly down the wall as Murphy backed out of the hall, and hid his smile behind another bite of bread. This would look good on his record.

NINE

The stairs creaked as Jason descended and he paused to listen. There was no sound from the back room where Mary slept. He moved downward again, stepping carefully over Murphy's muddy boots he had discarded in the entryway.

Jason sighed as the door clicked closed behind him. The weak yellow glow of the street lights attempted to push back the thick darkness that filled the street as Jason hurried down the empty sidewalk. Someone was waiting at the corner up ahead, just out of the circle of light from the streetlight.

"Who's there?" Jason called softly. He knew it had to be one of Jarris' men.

"It's me," Benjamin replied coming toward him. "I wanted to make sure you were not late."

"Thanks." Jason walked past him. "I think I can handle it."

"Don't be childish, Roper." Benjamin told him. "So you got into a little hot water, Silas let you off easy, so let it go."

"Thanks for the advice." Jason allowed Benjamin to fall in beside him. "What are you, my nanny?"

"Hey, I got my job, you got yours," Benjamin answered. Jason thought of Kirk, and fell silent. He wondered where Kirk was now.

"Dude, let it go. You and I got to stick together."

"I wasn't even thinking about that," Jason told him.

"What were you thinking about?" Benjamin seemed genuinely curious.

"You can report my movements to Frank and Silas, but not my thoughts. Those are my own."

"Fine, be cagey." Benjamin lowered his voice. They could see the Taylor's sign up ahead.

"Have you ever been to a raid?" Jason asked in a whisper. "I mean what are we expected to do?"

"You and I, and a few others, will do a little vandalism inside while Gary and Frank rough up the manager a bit." Benjamin whispered back ducking around the corner onto a smaller one way street. "There won't be any guns or anything since this is just the raid. If Taylor doesn't pull out by Wednesday, we will strike again for keeps."

They approached a small group of men who stood quietly in the shadows.

"Is everyone here?"

Jason could not see the men's faces but he recognized the voice as Frank's. Someone passed out dark ski caps to each of them. Jason followed their example and slid it over his face.

"You four take the store," Frank continued in a low voice. "Destroy whatever you want, make it look bad. Toby you and Colby go for the expensive items, the TVs and such. Benjamin and Roper, just tear up as much as possible. We have twenty minutes max so let's do a good job."

The men nodded silently and Jason was handed a thick stick. He tested the weight of it in his hand. Benjamin bumped him playfully.

"You ready for this?"

Jason grinned in the darkness, "You bet." Inside he was cringing. He saw no way to stop the operation, no way to warn Mr. Taylor. All he could do was pray that the police had received his message.

They crept toward the entrance. A dim light was on by the office, but the rest of the store was relatively dark. The only other light came from the emergency exit lights that reflected an eerie red on the well-polished floor. Toby pulled out a little pouch and set to work on the lock. In minutes he pushed it open and the gang flooded the store each hurrying to accomplish the part assigned to him. They had not made it past the line of checkout counters when the store lights came on. Three cops appeared out of nowhere creating a tight semi circle around the intruders. The officers kept their guns trained on them. Officer Wayne Rimbowlt took over, barking orders like a drill sergeant.

"Get together. Back up, you. Don't try anything, we've got you covered."

Looking around, Jason noticed that Toby was not with them. Somehow he had made it past the officers and was somewhere in the store. Jason knew there was no way he could inconspicuously protect all three officers without blowing his cover. He moved with the group racking his mind for a way to escape.

Colby moved a little more toward the door. "I got two strikes against me already," Jason heard him whisper. "If they take me for this, I won't get out for years."

"We aren't done yet," Gary growled.

"Keep quiet," Wayne commanded firmly. "Get your hands up on that wall."

Taylor came out of his office, gun in hand. "Good work, officers."

Without warning Gary jerked a gun out from under his jacket, and pointed it at Taylor. Jason turned, placing himself in the line of fire, as Gary squeezed the trigger. He moved just enough to stop the bullet without it being obvious that it had hit him. The bullet disappeared, missing its mark completely and went unnoticed in the commotion that followed. Joe's gun barked, the bullet crashing through the thick glass door inches away from Gary's head. Seeing his chance, Colby made a break for it, and this time it was

Wayne's gun that answered the challenge. Colby cried out in pain and fell to the ground clutching his leg.

"Anyone else?" Wayne asked, looking at each one in turn. No one met his challenge and the store was suddenly deathly quiet except for the moans from Colby.

Benjamin's eyes were locked on Colby and Jason saw fear in his expression.

"Dustin, call for backup, and get an ambulance here as well." Wayne covered for him as the officer moved out of combat to radio in the call. "You guys get your hands on that wall."

Jason noticed Gary was staring at him and tried hard not to meet his eyes. Gary's bullet had not hit its mark because Jason had been in the way, and he could tell Gary was sorting out the facts in his head.

They moved to the wall and put their hands on it well above their heads.

"Alright, drop your guns." Toby's strong voice echoed in the empty store.

The officers spun around to see Toby holding a gun to Dustin's head. His elbow was hooked under Dustin's chin keeping the officer close against himself as he moved toward them.

The officers hesitated then bent and laid their guns onto the floor.

"Grab 'em, Frank." Toby ordered.

Frank obeyed handing the guns out to his men.

"Get him out of here," Toby directed them with a quick glance at Colby.

Benjamin and Jason hurried to obey. They carried him out and maneuvered him into the back of the SUV that was to have served as their getaway car. Gary and Frank came out about ten minutes later, looking overly pleased with themselves. They hopped into the car and started the motor.

Toby backed out of the store, his gun still trained on someone inside. He jumped into the car and Gary hit the gas. Jason and Benjamin clung to the seats and to Colby, trying to keep him as still as possible. Gary sped through the streets turning off on numerous one way streets, paying little or no attention to the signs that marked them. They squealed to a stop outside a car garage, Toby and Frank scrambled out and opened the big garage door. Gary pulled in and they slid the door closed once more, locking it into place.

Gary climbed out of the driver's seat wearing a heavy scowl. "What I want to know is how the cops knew we were going to be there?"

"Somebody tipped them off," Frank fumed, pacing the dark garage.

"Colby's hurt bad, isn't he?"

Jason looked up at Toby. He was a tall dark man, his thick hair was cut short and there was a hint of refinement in the way he carried himself. "Yeah, it's pretty bad. Is there somewhere we can take him?"

Toby thought for a moment. "There is, if we can get him in without being seen."

"He's already lost a lot of blood, we've got to get him help soon or he's not going to make it," Jason told them. He was kneeling in the floor beside the back seat where Colby was sprawled unconscious.

Frank jerked open the side door. "You talked to the cops." He pointed an accusing finger at Jason. "I knew Silas let you off too easily."

"I don't think this is a time to go pointing fingers," Jason shot back. "If you think back you'll remember that I didn't even know when, or where, we were meeting until after you're little interrogation about the police thing, so lay off. Toby, where do we take him?"

"The apartments. No one ever checks the rooms there.

If we can get him up to my room I could hide him out there for a while."

"Good, let's go."

"I'm not through with you, Roper," Frank threatened. "I know you're the one behind this, and I'm going to prove it."

"This isn't the time, Frank. Colby got it worse than you tonight so let it rest," Toby told him, taking the keys from Gary. "We'll meet with Silas and figure this thing out. Maybe they just didn't catch the leak in time over at the station."

Jason kept a straight face as if what he was hearing was nothing new. He had guessed the police were involved with Jarris to a certain extent. What he needed to find out now was how deeply the corruption ran.

"I've got something to bring up as well," Gary told Jason, toying with the gun in his hand.

Jason looked back at him without flinching. He knew exactly how to worm his way out of this one.

"We'll let Silas sort it out," Toby told them, his tone made it final. "Gary, I think it would be best to hide the car for a while just in case the police got the tags."

Gary nodded sullenly. "I'll drop you off and take care of it tonight."

Toby tossed him the keys and jumped in the passenger seat. "Frank, grab the door."

Frank slid it up and checked the street before giving them the all clear. Gary eased the car out of the garage into the darkness.

"You guys have a doctor, right?" Jason asked as they sped silently through the dimly lit streets.

"No, Kernigan was the only one who knew a little about doctoring. I have his stuff at my place, and you're welcome to use whatever you need."

"What do you mean?" Jason asked turning to look at him.

"You've had some medical training." Toby grinned at

Jason's surprised look "You didn't think I could tell?"

"I guess I never thought about it," Jason answered, bracing against Colby as they turned another corner.

"Easy on the corners, Gary. You are slinging Colby all over the place." Benjamin steadied the wounded man's head and glanced at Jason. "He's going to make it right?"

Jason shrugged. "I can't make any promises at this point. But I'll do my best."

———

"You shot Roper?" Silas asked obviously surprised.

"He didn't shoot me, Mr. Silas. His bullet went by me and for some reason he's convinced it went through me or something. I told you he'd be amazed by anything since he thinks I am still 'wet behind the ears.'" Jason glared at Gary to emphasize his point.

"I tell you the bullet didn't go on after it hit him. It just disappeared," Gary insisted.

"What are you trying to say?" Silas asked leaning back in his chair.

"I don't know what happened, but if Roper here hadn't been in the way. Taylor would not be alive or at least he would be seriously wounded."

"You are blaming that on me?" Jason was playing up the defensive. "The truth is you missed. Don't go blaming that on me."

"Gentlemen, I really don't see a point to all this," Silas interrupted. "Gary, the invincible angle is a bit far fetched. It is more likely that you simply misjudged the angle."

Gary crossed his muscular arms and glared at Jason, but he did not argue any further.

"I am guessing you took the time to rough Taylor up a bit?"

"Yeah, we delivered the message," Frank answered with a cruel grin.

"And Roper." Silas met his eyes. "Toby told me you took care of Colby. I didn't know you had medical training."

"Yes, Sir. Colby is stable for now. Toby said he'd stay with him tonight, that's why he's not here."

"Then the night was not wasted. I'll get this trouble with the police sorted out and we will be back in business. You have all had a stressful night, I suggest you go home, blow off some steam, or sleep it off, whatever. I'll contact you sometime tomorrow, or the day after."

Frank was the first to rise. "Alright, you heard him, clear out."

Benjamin left quickly; glad to be out of the tense and stuffy room. Gary glared at Jason, then rose and stormed out without a word. Jason was at the door when Silas called him back.

"Sit down, Roper. I need to have a word with you. Frank, I'll meet with you first thing tomorrow morning. We've got to sort out some things, before we move again."

Frank nodded and left, giving Jason a warning look as he passed.

Silas closed the door and returned to his seat behind the desk. "Roper, Jarris has allowed you to be overly bold with me and my men up to this point. Mr. Jarris likes a little fire in his men, and I do too, but I think we let you go too far because we both knew you wouldn't cross us."

Jason didn't meet his eyes.

"I want you to know that I am raising the bar for you. I will no longer tolerate any disrespect or arguing from you. Is that clear?"

"Yes, Sir," Jason mumbled.

"I am doing this for your own good," Silas went on. His tone reminded Jason of speeches his dad had given him when he had not lived up to his father's expectations. "Some of my men don't appreciate the airs you put on. I know you feel invincible at this age, but it would be safer to tone it down a bit."

"Gary had it out for me from the first," Jason told him. "He just looked at me and hated me."

"It's not just Gary, Roper. There are others who are… irritated, by your behavior. Your turning up in strange places and talking over things with people you shouldn't, doesn't help them trust you any more."

Jason nodded. "I understand. I'll be more careful in the future."

"Good." Silas rose. "I'll send Frank for you when we are moving again. He will give you your next assignment."

Jason hesitated at the door.

"Is there something else?" Silas asked.

Jason turned to face Silas once more. "I know I've only been with this operation for a few days…" Silas waited for him to finish.

Jason shifted uncomfortably. "Well, it's just that the pay isn't so good."

"You've got free room and board." Silas reminded him. "If you'd take it."

Jason nodded. "I know."

"Just spit it out, Roper. I don't have time to draw it out of you."

Jason stood taller, he despised being treated like a child. "I am considering getting a job on the side, to get a little spare cash."

"Where?"

"There is an opening at that little diner next to that big office building on the corner of Parkway and Roger. I was thinking of applying there since I didn't see myself getting hired on at Taylor's."

Silas grinned. "You do have brains after all."

Jason waited.

"I don't see that being a problem, Roper, as long as it doesn't get in the way of your real job."

"All the real gigs have been at night so it shouldn't be a problem. If I take the day shifts, I'll get off by eight at the latest and no one will have any reason to suspect I am involved with any of it."

"Afraid of spoiling your record?" Silas asked.

"I like to play it safe," Jason responded, careful to keep the irritation he felt out of his voice.

"Sounds like you've got yourself another job. I'd give it a week or so to let this thing cool off, but Toby knows some people at the diner if you have trouble getting in."

"Thanks." Jason left the office and headed for Mary's, hoping to get some rest.

The sky was a pale gray when he reached the house. He let himself in, setting Murphy's boots up by the wall before heading up the stairs to his room. He closed and locked the door and then flopped down on the bed. His mind spun through the night's events, he thought of what he could have done and what he might have needed to do as he lay there alone in the darkness. The first rays of morning light were creeping across the sky when he finally drifted off into a fitful sleep.

T EN

A soft but urgent knock drew Jason's attention from the damp shirt he was hanging up to dry. It had been almost a week since he had heard from any of the gang. He tossed the shirt on the bed. Moving quickly he crossed the room and stood against the wall beside the door.

"Who is it?" he asked quietly.

"Benjamin."

Jason unlocked the door and Benjamin squeezed in, shutting it quickly behind him.

"What are you doing here?" Jason asked, retrieving the damp shirt from the bed.

"You know how you are always complaining that I rat on you?" Benjamin asked checking the window to make sure no one was watching them.

"Yeah." Jason slid the shirt onto a hanger and hung it on the rod in the closet.

"Well, you aren't the only one I keep tabs on." Benjamin's face betrayed a mixture of fear and anger as he turned his attention back to Jason. "Gary's gunning for you, Roper. He's dead set that that bullet went through you and he's out to prove it."

"You're kidding." Jason knew by the look in Benjamin's eyes that he wasn't. "That was nearly a week ago."

"I came to let you know. You'd better steer clear of him best you can for a while, at least until he cools off."

"Thanks, Benjamin. I really mean it."

"What are friends for?" Benjamin asked with a weak smile.

Jason checked the hall then moved so Benjamin could slip out. Benjamin briefly touched his finger tips to his forehead and then disappeared down the stairs.

———

"You want me to hire you?" The balding man folded his arms on the high counter and looked Jason over. "What experience do you have?"

"I'm willing to learn whatever it takes," Jason answered, looking around the crowded place. "I mean I know pretty much what servers do."

The owner shrugged. "I am short on help. I guess I can give you a try." He disappeared into the back room and returned with an application. "You can use that table over there."

"Thanks." Jason took the application and looked it over as he walked.

He sat down then realized he did not have a pen. He patted his pockets in search of one.

"Here."

Jason looked up to see Officer Wayne sitting at the next table over, he was holding a pen. Jason froze, if the officer remembered him and took him in that would be the end of everything. Jason made himself take the pen. "Thank you, Sir."

Wayne looked at him and Jason knew the cop was piecing it together. He leaned over the application filling in the blanks as quickly as possible. Under scrutiny he was having trouble remembering his new information. Jason pulled out his license and copied the information it gave. He looked up at the ceiling trying hard to remember the new social security number his dad had assigned him.

"You were at Taylor's last week." Wayne said without emotion.

Their eyes locked for a moment, and Jason looked away.

"I think you've got the wrong guy," Jason told him. He remembered the number and jotted it down.

Wayne watched, silently sipping his coffee now and then, as Jason sweated over the application. After what seemed like ages, Jason stood and walked to the counter without so much as a glance at the officer.

"Here you go, Mr. Weaver."

"That was quick." The owner looked it over, running a hand across the bald spot on top of his head. "It seems to be in order. There is a possibility of a background check. Would there be any reason you wouldn't want that done?"

Jason shrugged. "I've got nothing to hide."

———

"I hear there was a cop talking to you at the diner." Toby watched as Jason tied off the bandage on Colby's leg.

"News sure does move fast around here." Jason put the scissors back into the bag and zipped it closed. "The cop started nosing around when I went in for an application. It's like I have a sign on me that says 'talk to me.'" He wadded up the bloodstained bandage and stuffed it into a plastic grocery bag, pulling off his disposable gloves before tying up the sack.

"What did he want?"

"He didn't say much really. Although at one point he thought he remembered me from Taylor's, I had the most terrible feeling in the pit of my stomach when he said that. It must have been how Colby felt when he thought he was going back for good."

"So did he remember you?"

"He didn't do anything, so I played it cool and got out of there as fast as I could."

"Was he one of the ones at Taylor's?

"Yeah, he was the guy in charge."

Toby nodded. "We'll have to keep an eye on him. Apparently he and his partner decided to go off on a personal mission without notifying the chief."

"Does that happen a lot?" Jason asked. He surveyed the room, there was nothing out of place that would show Colby had been wounded, except for Colby himself who was unnaturally pale.

"It has happened once or twice, but never to that extent. If I hadn't been so far in when they ambushed us we'd probably all be in the slammer. We will have to be careful not to let that happen again."

"So, the cops have to act under the chief's orders at all times?"

"That's right. That is how we have been able to do so well."

"So the chief is on our side."

"I didn't say that," Toby informed him firmly. "Mr. Jarris is just very good at avoiding trouble with the police in this area."

"I can tell," Jason agreed, moving the conversation back into safer waters. "He's got this whole town under his thumb."

Toby smiled, "Yeah, he's a great leader."

Jason frowned. "Toby, there's something I've been wondering."

"What's that?"

"What ever happened to Edgar?"

Toby met his eyes. "Jarris is a good leader, Roper. Edgar crossed him one too many times, so he got what was coming to him. Leave it at that."

Jason nodded and dropped the subject. He gave Toby a few last minute instructions on Colby's care, and then slipped out and strolled nonchalantly down the sidewalk without a backward glance.

———

"Jason, there's someone here to see you," Mary called

up the stairs.

"Coming." Jason told her. She always insisted on using his first name, and he didn't have the guts to argue with her about it. He pulled on a gray collared shirt over his t-shirt and quickly smoothed his hair in the mirror. Grabbing his gun off the dresser he checked the ammunition clip and then slipped it into the side pocket of his cargo pants. Picking up the blue apron from the desk, Jason unlocked and opened the door.

He heard Murphy's door open as he reached the bottom of the stairs. "I have to be at work in five minutes so you'd better…" Jason stopped cold. The visitor was not Frank. It was a cop in full uniform. Jason recognized him from the raid at Taylor's.

"I'm sorry I was expecting someone else. Can I help you?" Jason asked politely.

"Are you Jason Roper?"

"Yes, Sir."

"I'm going to need you to come with me to the station."

"I believe I have the right to know why," Jason answered respectfully.

"Suspicion of breaking and entering, and gang involvement," Dustin told him bluntly.

"Today's my first day on the job. I won't have a chance if I'm picked up for questioning and am late my first day."

"You should have thought of that before you went to Taylor's," Dustin replied opening the front door. "Let's go."

"I have an alibi," Jason told him glancing at his clock.

"Let's hear it." He shut the door again and crossed his arms.

"Murphy?" Jason yelled up the stairs. "Do you mind being my alibi?"

"What for?" Murphy came down the stairs. Jason had never seen him so alert. "Afternoon, Officer."

"I'm going to be late for work but he says I was over

burglarizing Taylor's last Thursday night."

"No, Sir. I think you've got the wrong guy. He and I were here all night. Mrs. Mary can vouch for that."

All eyes turned to Mary who shrugged. "I can't deny it. I did hear them both go to bed and they were both up there when I got up that next morning."

"How is it you remember that night so well?" Dustin asked suspiciously.

"I had just had a long talk with Jason and I had trouble going to sleep that night. I remember hearing Jason up there pacing around for a long time, and I remember thinking to myself "He's got a lot on his mind for such a young boy." But he quit pacing about an hour before I went to bed. Other than Murphy's snoring the place was quiet all night."

"Will you sign a statement for me?" Dustin asked knowing he was outnumbered. "Both of you."

"I'd be glad to," Murphy answered without hesitation.

"Am I free to go?" Jason asked. Glancing at his watch and edging toward the door.

"For now, but I may be back if I need any additional information."

"Thanks for understanding," Jason slid out the door and hurried away from the house. That was way too close.

Eleven

"Hey, how's it going?"

Jason looked up from the dirty dishes he was stacking, and a bead of sweat trickled down his face. "It's going. I get my first paycheck tomorrow which is about all that is keeping me going today."

Benjamin grinned. "Welcome to the life of the common Joe."

"Thanks, Benjamin." Jason pretended to be irritated. He grinned and shook his head as he put the last of the dishes into his plastic tub. "How about you? Do you have a normal life on the side?" Jason asked wiping down the table with a soapy rag.

"Nah, I'm happy where I am."

Jason looked up at him and smiled. "Sure" He hefted the bin and headed for the kitchen. "I'll be back out in a minute."

When he returned Benjamin was sitting at one of the dirty tables. He slapped it impatiently. "Server, get this mess cleaned up."

Jason bowed slightly. "Yes Sir, right away, Sir."

Benjamin laughed. "Do you take orders too?"

"Nope, I'm a lowly 'hopper." Jason started clearing the table.

Benjamin shook his head sadly. "What a shame." Benjamin glanced up "Better watch out, here comes the tyrant," he whispered.

Jason looked up to see Mr. Weaver coming toward them. "Hi, Mr. Weaver."

"Mr. Roper." Mr. Weaver folded his arms. "I think I made it clear that you are not to spend work time socializing."

"Hey." Benjamin stood to face him. "He's working isn't he?"

"Benjamin." Jason's tone carried a warning.

Benjamin glanced at him and dropped the subject. "Alright, I guess I'll see you tonight."

"Sure, Benjamin. See ya." Jason turned his attention back to Mr. Weaver. "I'm sorry sir. I didn't think you would mind if I talked while I worked."

"Well, I do." Mr. Weaver answered sternly. "Don't let it happen again."

"I won't, Sir." Jason turned back to the table with a tired sigh. The day stretched on for what seemed like forever. The hands of the clock on the wall crawled so slowly toward eight that several times Jason was sure they had stopped moving altogether.

"It's twenty minutes till closing time," one of the waitresses told Jason with a smile. "We're almost out of here."

Jason gave her a tired smile. "Thanks, Angie." He had two more tables to clean. The diner was empty and Jason hoped it would stay that way until closing time. He came out of the kitchen and stopped, his wet rag dripping on the dirty floor. There was Officer Wayne sitting comfortably at one of the clean tables.

"Watch the rag," Angie warned passing him to take the cop's order.

Jason wadded it up and went to the table he was finishing. Wayne had positioned himself right beside the other dirty table and Jason knew it was not by accident. He glanced at the clock, the cop still had 15 minutes. Jason returned to the kitchen. Wayne was probably there fishing for a tip, but Jason couldn't afford to give him one at this point. There were too many things hanging on the edge right now. If Jason gave him a tip it would confirm the suspicions of the guys who were watching him, just waiting for him to slip up.

"There's one more table, Jason."

Jason glanced at Amy, a pretty young waitress who had been working at Weaver's for two years already. "I know. I'm getting to it."

"Just don't let Mr. Weaver catch you back here taking a break on his time."

"He needs to get off my back." Jason caught himself and sighed angrily. "I'm sorry, Amy, I shouldn't have said that." He could not afford to lose this job.

"It's been a long day," she answered going back to her work.

Jason took a deep breath and let it out slowly before pushing open the swinging door. He set the tub on a chair and started clearing the table.

"Dustin told me you squirmed out of his interrogation last week." Wayne did not bother with pleasantries.

Jason shrugged, "I wasn't there and could prove it."

"You and I both know you were there," Wayne told him, keeping his voice low enough that the waitresses would not overhear.

"I'm really not supposed to talk to customers while I'm working," Jason told the officer, his voice carried well in the empty diner.

"The only reason you are still out is because of me, I need you on the outside."

Jason clenched his teeth, but said nothing. He wiped the table down with more force than was necessary.

"I have a feeling there's something coming up real soon," Wayne prompted.

"You won't get anything from me," Jason told him with an angry glare. He lifted the bin of dishes and carried it off to the kitchen.

"What was that about?" Mr. Weaver was on him before he had a chance to set the dishes down.

"Nothing," Jason muttered.

"It didn't look like 'nothing' to me," Mr. Weaver pressed.

Looking past Weaver, Jason took a deep breath and let it out slowly. Amy caught his eye and shook her head warningly. "Play it cool," she mouthed.

"Okay. I'll level with you." Jason propped the dish bin on the counter. "He wants me to play the spy for him with some of the diner customers. I've told him I can't. I've told him I won't, but he just keeps pestering."

"I'll have a word with him," Mr. Weaver left the kitchen and Jason could tell he was riled.

"What's the grin for?" Angie asked. She was on her way to refill Wayne's coffee cup.

Jason shrugged, still grinning and started emptying the bin. He was tempted to move where he could see what was happening, but held back. He had played his hand well, now he needed to play it safe.

"That's it. We are done!" Angie dumped the coffee and set the empty coffee pot on the counter. Let's get this place cleaned up and get out of here."

"You got anything tonight, Jason?" Amy asked.

"Yeah, I'm meeting up with a buddy of mine."

"Good, you need to get out and blow some steam."

Jason turned back to the sink to hide his amusement. If she only knew.

"What about you, Amy? Any big plans for this fine Friday night?" Angie poured hot water into the mop bucket.

"Yeah, me and Ted are going to the late show tonight."

"Sounds fun."

"I've done my part, I'm out of here." The cook told them taking off his grimy apron.

"Thanks, Jeff, have a nice weekend."

"You too." He tossed his apron into the laundry bin on his way out the back door.

Angie and Amy put the chairs up on the tables while Jason mopped the floor. They waited, chatting in the back until Jason had finished. It was after nine when they finally locked up for the night.

Jason walked briskly toward Mary's, unable to keep the grin off his face.

"You look like you won the lottery," Benjamin commented. He was leaning against the rail of Mary's porch.

"I practically did." Jason slapped him on the back. "Come on up and I'll tell you about it. I've got to change before we head out."

Benjamin followed him up the stairs.

"What's all this?" Murphy asked skeptically, a ham sandwich sagging limply in his hand.

"Jason won the lottery," Benjamin told him with a grin.

"What?"

"I got that pesky cop back good," Jason told him hanging his apron on the closet door.

"Alright, let's hear the story." Benjamin seated himself on the bed and Murphy stood in the doorway still munching his sandwich.

"Well, you both know that Officer Wayne has been hanging around the diner a lot, just pestering me."

"Yeah."

Jason pulled off his gray shirt straightened the black shirt he had worn beneath. "Well, tonight I got a little riled and Mr. Weaver noticed."

"That man is such a pain."

"That's beside the point," Jason told him tucking in his shirt. He hesitated. There was not a way to discreetly put on his holster. He would have to wait until he was alone.

"So he asked about it?" Murphy prompted.

"Yeah, and I just about lost it with him." Jason ran a comb through his dark hair. "But then I had this brilliant idea so I 'leveled with him'. I told him the cop had been trying to get me to spy on some of the customers and give him information about them. I played it up real good and sounded so noble it made me sick."

Benjamin laughed. "What did Ol' Weaver do?"

"Oh, he was mad. He went out there and gave the cop a large piece of his mind. It took every bit of self-control I had to keep from peeking out to see the show."

"I sure wish I could have been there." Benjamin shook his head, "What a sight that must have been."

Jason pretended to wipe the grin from his face. "Alright boys, let's move."

"Is it time already?" Benjamin asked turning the digital clock around. "Hey, it's unplugged."

"Yeah, I don't use it much," Jason told him. "It's 9:30."

"Wow, we'd better get out of here." They hurried down the stairs and almost ran into Mary.

"Where are you boys off to?" she knew better than to ask but did anyway.

"We're going to the late show," Jason lied cheerfully. "Man, I forgot my jacket. I'll meet you out front."

"Alright, but hurry or we'll be late and they'll start the movie without us."

Jason felt like he had been grinning all night. He raced up the stairs kicking the door closed behind him and quickly strapped on his holster. It felt good to have the gun tight against him once more. He pulled on his jacket and hurried down the stairs and out into the dusky street.

Jason Roper

TWELVE

"Benjamin, that's Frank isn't it? Two blocks up."

Benjamin glanced ahead then nodded. "Yeah, that's him."

"He's being tailed," Jason observed, keeping his eyes on closer objects.

"Hmm." Benjamin paused to examine some graffiti on a brick wall. "Can you tell who it is?"

"I'm guessing a cop. But he's not in uniform."

Benjamin started walking again. "So it's another 'cops day off raid.'"

"How do we tell him?" Jason asked.

"Easy." Benjamin stooped and picked up a few white pebbles from a flowerbed. "I'll run ahead and put these in his path."

"And he'll know what that means?" Jason asked.

"Sure, just watch." Benjamin cut off down a side street, when he reached a parallel street he sprinted out of sight.

Jason was so focused on seeing Benjamin emerge up ahead of Frank that he did not notice the officer until he was right beside him.

"Out for an evening stroll?"

"You cops have something against that now?" Jason asked without stopping.

The policeman fell in beside him. "No, not really. What are you looking for?"

"I don't really see how that is any of your business."

Jason answered. "But I'm meeting up with a friend to go to a movie tonight."

"Is it any good?"

"I don't know, I haven't gone yet." Jason saw Frank stop and kick at something on the sidewalk.

"You know him?"

"Who, my friend?" Jason asked glancing at the cop beside him.

The man gestured at Frank. "Him."

"It's kind of dark to tell but I'm pretty sure I don't."

Benjamin approached looking pleased with himself. "It worked like a charm. Evening, Officer."

"Good evening."

"So you convinced her to let you go?"

Benjamin smiled. "Yeah, she feels sorry for me never getting to have 'guy time'. How lame is that."

"What time does the late show start?" Jason asked, ignoring the officer beside them.

"Ten, I think" Benjamin replied. "Isn't that right, officer?"

"Yeah, I think it does start at ten."

"How come you get a personal escort and I've got to come alone?" Benjamin complained.

"I'm one of those important people," Jason told him.

"Some day that will be me," Benjamin replied with longing in his voice.

Jason did his best to hide his smile. "He's a singer." He told the cop, ignoring the surprised look Benjamin tried to disguise as modesty.

"Really? Well let's hear some."

"I don't just sing out on the street for anybody," Benjamin told him.

Frank approached them going the opposite direction.

"Besides, we will have to hurry to make it to the ten o'clock show," Benjamin added for Frank to hear. Frank did not show any sign of recognition as he brushed past them.

"Can't you sing while you walk?" the officer asked, nodding slightly to the second man who approached them.

"Excuse me," Jason caught the man's arm as he passed. "Do you mind sticking around for just a minute? See Scott here is a big singer and he doesn't ever sing for crowds smaller than three."

"Actually I…"

"Great. It will only take a few minutes. You can spare that much time can't you?"

The undercover policeman looked desperately past them and Jason could tell by his face that he had lost sight of Frank.

He sighed. "I guess I've got time now."

"Good, go for it Scotty."

"You forgot." Benjamin told him seriously. "I never sing for less than twenty bucks."

"Twenty?! Are you mad?" the cop exclaimed. "That's ridiculous."

"Then I can't sing," Benjamin told them. "Come on, we're going to be late."

"You don't know what you are missing." Jason strode after Benjamin. They left the officers conferring on the sidewalk and hurried to the theater.

"Dude, that was awesome." Benjamin laughed when they were sure the cops weren't following. "I thought I was really going to have to sing for a while there."

Jason chuckled. "I did too. Hey if we get a ticket and make sure Amy sees us at the theater we'll have a pretty good alibi for tonight."

"You got money?"

"Sure, Toby loaned me some a few days ago." Jason patted his pocket.

"That sounds good to me. But we've got to make it fast."

———

"What took you so long?" Gary demanded. "Silas said ten sharp not ten thirty."

"We were trailed," Benjamin replied quietly.

"I told you they were going to be a little late," Frank reminded him. "Taylor's light went out about fifteen minutes ago. We'll give him about five more before we move in."

"What do I need to do?" Jason asked quietly.

"Hey, we'll tell you when we're ready to," Gary snapped.

Jason didn't respond. They waited in silence outside the dark house.

"Frank." Benjamin whispered. "You should have seen Roper today. He talked all three of us out of trouble. Those cops thought they were something trailing us and all and we left them puzzling over what to do."

"Good," Frank answered without any sign of pleasure, and Benjamin fell silent.

"Let's go," Toby hissed coming from behind the house. "The kid is in the back bedroom. His bed is to the left of the window."

"We're not hurting his kid are we?" Jason asked.

"Why, does that bother you?" Gary sneered at him.

"Lay off, Gary," Toby warned. "Roper we're just taking him for a bit. Just so he knows we are serious."

Jason nodded. "Okay, I don't mind roughing up a grown man but kids are out of my league."

"That's fine. You will be the lookout anyway." Toby handed him a walkie-talkie. "Beep it once if we need to clear out." He handed out black ski masks and everyone pulled one on.

They moved silently away toward the house.

"Don't botch this one," Frank told him in a low voice. "If we don't get him out, we'll know who to blame."

"I'll do my job," Jason told him.

They left Jason beside the porch and crept forward. Toby

pulled out his tools, the door opened under his experienced hand, and they disappeared inside the house. Something moved in the darkness close to the house next door and Jason felt cold fear trickle down his neck. He beeped the walkie-talkie.

To the right he saw something else move across the street. He could not make it out, but he knew something or someone was moving in the blackness. "Use the back door," Jason hissed into the walkie-talkie. "We've got company out here." Headlights lit up a house a few doors down as a car stopped at the corner before slowly turning down the street toward Taylor's house. Inside he heard a muffled child's cry. Jason ducked inside the house.

"Toby?" Jason called in a barely audible whisper. Someone touched him and he almost jumped out of his skin.

"It's me," Benjamin told him softly. "This way."

Jason could just make out the struggling form of a child in Gary's strong arms. Gary had a hand clamped over the kid's mouth and the boy's eyes were wide with terror. "We've got to get out of here," Jason told them urgently. "This place is crawling with cops."

"What?" Frank hissed.

"Where are they?" Toby asked moving to the window and carefully peering out.

"There was someone by the neighbor's house." Jason pointed to show them where. "And something else was moving on the other side as well. Plus there's a…"

The lights of the car passed over the front yard and came to rest on the front door.

"Car," Jason finished weakly.

All eyes turned to Toby.

"Split up and get out as you can. Make it fast. If they decide to surround us we'll use the kid to get us out."

Benjamin went to the door but Jason put a hand on his

arm. "Let me go first."

Benjamin nodded silently, not looking forward to this gamble with death.

Jason slipped out silently and almost ran into an officer on the back porch. The man would have sounded the alarm but Jason punched him in the stomach, knocking the wind out of him. Before he knew what was happening, the cop's gun was out, and a little burst of flame appeared in the darkness as the bullet shot out of the barrel two inches from Jason's chest.

Jason's fist connected with the man's jaw and he stumbled back, stumbling on the stairs and falling to the ground. Jason dove for the house once more.

"We're going to have to use the kid," Jason panted, "and make a run for it."

Gary hooked his arm under one of the boy's and across his little chest taking hold of his other arm so he would have a free hand. "If you make one noise I'll blow your head off," Gary told the kid, and his voice sent a chill through Jason. "Get it?" The boy's eyes were huge and tears were starting to trickle down his little face. Gary slowly removed his hand from the boy's mouth, and the kid did not make a sound except for shaky little sobs that he could not control.

"You're a brave kid," Jason told him softly.

"Let's go." Toby handed Gary a gun. "He's no use to us if he's dead." He reminded him sternly.

"Come out with your hands up," a man outside commanded loudly.

"We've got the kid," Gary bellowed back putting the gun to the little boy's head. "You shoot and he's dead."

Upstairs a woman screamed something about her baby.

"You stay up there and keep quiet, and he won't get hurt," Frank yelled up the stairs keeping them covered just in case.

"Alright, I'm coming out with the kid. Keep your distance."

Gary stepped out onto the back porch.

The officer Jason had tangled with backed slowly away as Gary emerged.

"Don't think about bumping me off either." Gary continued walking boldly down the porch steps. "If you shoot me one of the others will take out the kid."

Toby and Frank stepped out, guns in hand, followed closely by Jason and Benjamin.

"Release the hostage." Jason recognized the commanding voice, it was Wayne.

"Don't try to follow," Gary warned cruelly. "Or the kid will get it."

Toby and Frank took up the front keeping their weapons ready as they moved across the yard toward Gary's car that was parked on the corner. Jason and Benjamin brought up the rear, keeping their backs to Gary and their guns toward the cops. Gary shoved the boy into the back seat and climbed in after him. The police stood watching helplessly as the gangsters got into the vehicle.

Toby shoved the pedal down hard and they sped off down the street.

————

Toby pulled up to the back of an old hotel.

"Gary, you and Benjamin take the kid up. Here's the room key. Benjamin, you are going to stay with him. Gary once you drop him off, get out of there as fast as possible. You did a lot of talking, and that cop is bound to recognize your voice if he hears it again. Lay low a while, I'll contact you when this cools off a bit."

Gary climbed out of the car and lugged the child to the side door of the hotel that had been left unlocked for this occasion. Benjamin checked the street, then pulled it open and they disappeared inside.

"Roper, get out here and make a beeline for the theater, cover for Benjamin and make sure that alibi of yours sticks."

Jason nodded and jumped out. He watched as the car sped away then ran down the dark street to the theater. Inside, the movie was just letting out. Jason quickly moved through the crowd along the wall and slipped back into the theater. He pulled an empty cup from the trash and stood on the ramp watching the credits roll.

"Hi Jason, how'd you like the show?" Amy asked coming down the ramp.

Jason read pleasure in her tone, and knew it had been good. "It was great. I thought I'd wait and see if there was anything after the credits."

"They don't usually put something on this kind of film," the guy with Amy told him. Jason assumed he must be Ted.

"Where's your friend?" Amy asked glancing around. "I hope you didn't have to come alone."

Jason gestured at the door with his cup. "He had to hit the restroom before we headed out."

Ted took Amy's hand. "Nice to meet you, Jason. Have a great night."

"Yeah, you too."

"See you Monday," Amy called over her shoulder.

Jason waited until the last people had trickled out of the theater then tossed the cup back into the trash and followed them out. His alibi was sealed.

THIRTEEN

"Hop in." Wayne held open the back door of the police car.

"I don't get why I have to ride to the station. Can't you just take my statement here?"

"No, you are a suspect for a kidnapping. I need to bring you in for questioning."

Jason looked at him for a moment, unimpressed, then shook his head and climbed in.

Jason tried the door when Wayne went around to the driver's side. It was locked.

He slumped back to wait looking as uninterested as possible.

Wayne put the car in gear.

"How did you know we were at Taylor's?" Jason asked with no change in his expression.

Wayne glanced at him in the review mirror and saw he was staring moodily out the window. "Just a hunch that paid off."

Jason threw up his hands as if he were angry. "How did you get past the chief?"

Wayne played along looking irritated as he pulled away from the curb. "The chief was out when we did the raid. He goes to some big meeting at M.C. Enterprises about every month or so."

Jason crossed his arms and slouched rebelliously to disguise his surprise. "M.C. Enterprises? In Burlington?" he asked with a sour look.

"One and the same." Wayne glanced at him in the mirror once more. "You know of it?"

"How do you know he goes there?" Jason asked with a shrug.

"We tailed him one time," Wayne answered without remorse.

"Did you find out who he meets with?"

"No. We have tailed him there twice, but the security is too tight for us to follow him in. We've got a connection on the other side who picks up the trail when he enters Burlington. He went in once posing as an art lover who was interested in a piece they had and said the elevator Lario got on went straight to the ninth floor. But that is as much as we have been able to find out so far."

Jason was silent.

"What about the kid?"

"I didn't know anything about it until I got there. I'll do my best to get him out, but its pretty touch and go right now. I'm not exactly a favorite with the guys. You showing up at the raids doesn't help much."

"I'm an officer. My job is to uphold the law and that's what I have to do." He pulled up to the curb in front of the station. "Can you tell me where he is?"

"Not at this point," Jason answered trying the door again and looking annoyed for the benefit of the people outside. "He's safe though."

Wayne got out and went around to Jason's door. He opened it and Jason got out.

"I'd advise you to be careful what you say," Wayne warned.

Jason had already guessed the place was bugged. He shrugged and walked begrudgingly through the station doors with Wayne right behind him.

———

"Roper."

Jason paused nonchalantly, as if deciding where to go next. "What is it?" he mumbled, leaning his shoulder against the brick wall to watch some kids playing ball across the street.

"What did they say?" Toby kicked at some trash in the alley, as if he had lost something.

"The alibi stuck," Jason responded, keeping his voice low. "The girl from Weaver's and her guy both signed the statement. They think the cop was just picking on me since I got him in trouble at the diner."

"Benjamin told me about that."

Jason could tell he was pleased.

"So are you clear?"

"Yes."

"Good. I need you to take Benjamin's place at the hotel for a couple of nights."

"I've got to be at work on Monday," Jason reminded him.

"I know, but you aren't the only one with a side job. Benjamin needs today and Sunday, and then he'll take it again early Monday morning. We need the kid alive which is why I'm not comfortable leaving him with Frank, or Gary, but he's still out for now."

"What time do you need me?"

"As soon as you can get there. The side door will be open," Toby replied. He strolled off down the street without another word. Jason waited a few minutes then took a roundabout route to the hotel. The door was open and Jason slipped in unnoticed. He climbed the stairs to the sixth floor, 602 was the first door on his right. He knocked and waited, watching the peek hole. Soon, he saw it go dark as Benjamin peered through, the deadbolt slid back and the door opened just enough to allow Jason to slip in.

"I'm glad he got you," Benjamin told him locking the door again. "So the alibi held?

"Yep, you and I are all the way in the clear."

"Good, I was afraid Frank would be the only one available."

"What about Murphy?" Jason asked.

"Murphy drinks too much," Benjamin answered picking up a pair of children's socks and tossing them around the corner. "He does little jobs here and there when he's sober, but I wouldn't want him to stay with the kid."

"Where is the kid?" Jason asked.

Benjamin moved further into the room and pointed to the little boy who was sleeping soundly on the full size bed. It was positioned so that couldn't be seen from the door. "He's a good kid," Benjamin told Jason.

"Don't worry, I'll take good care of him."

"You think I'm soft, don't you?" Benjamin asked searching Jason's face.

"No. I don't like this any more than you do." Jason looked around. "Anything I need to know?"

"We've got food here." Benjamin crossed the room to the little kitchenette and opened the mini refrigerator. "Milk, yogurt, jelly. There's mac n' cheese in the cabinet here, and bread and peanut butter."

"Looks like kid heaven," Jason told him with a smile.

"I wanted to make it less traumatic if possible," Benjamin told him glancing at the boy. "I figure some good food he likes would help."

"The key is there on the counter. But Toby said not to go anywhere just in case he starts crying or something." Benjamin slipped on his shoes and looked around the room once more. "I guess that's it. Have fun."

"What's his name?" Jason asked as Benjamin unlocked the door.

"Zach," Benjamin replied before slipping out.

Jason locked the door behind him and wandered around the hotel room. It was sparsely decorated but nice. The bathroom was on the left when you walked in then the room widened out. The full bed the boy was on was around the corner. A small kitchenette took up the far left corner. Out of habit Jason turned the digital clock to the wall on his way to the window; he could tell they hadn't picked the room for its view. He sat on the couch and looked over at the boy who was stirring in his sleep.

Jason ran a hand through his hair and sighed. Somehow he knew his dad was connected to the gang's movements but he didn't want to know how. Not yet anyway. The boy cried out in his sleep and Jason went to the bed. He stood there a minute undecided then sat carefully beside the boy and patted his back awkwardly. How could his dad be running a gang? He had always been so for justice and had trained Jason to think the same way, and now…Jason shook his head. This wasn't a good time for this. He needed time to think it out. To try to piece together what he had thought was real. To find out what was real, and what was just a front.

"Who are you?" the boy asked fearfully as he sat up and scooted away from Jason.

"I'm just somebody who is watching you." Jason guessed the boy was around six or seven years old.

"You're one of the bad men," Zach told him fiercely climbing out of the tangle of covers. "I want to go home."

"Well, you can't go yet. First your dad has to obey the… people and close his store."

"Why does he have to close it? My daddy likes his store," Zach demanded.

"Yeah, but these other people are trying to do something and your dad won't cooperate."

"My daddy says he doesn't have to listen to a bunch of thugs."

Jason stood. "Well, sometimes thugs get rough and have to be obeyed."

"Like when they gave my daddy a black eye and made his lip bleed?" Zach challenged.

"Yeah, like that. So if your dad will listen then you will get to go home."

"Do you do what thugs tell you?"

Jason thought about it for a moment then nodded. "I guess I do."

"Then you're bad," Zach told him louder than necessary climbing off the bed. "I'm going to run away." He made a beeline for the door but Jason easily cut him off.

He struggled, hitting Jason with his tiny fists. Jason held on to him and the child soon melted in his arms, tears streaming down his face and sobs racking his tiny frame.

"Are you done?" Jason asked.

Zach just cried.

Jason lifted him onto the bed and let him go. "I bet you feel better."

Zach hid his face in the covers his little shoulders shaking.

"So how about some breakfast?" Jason asked after Zach's sobs had diminished.

The boy faced him angrily. "I already ate breakfast with the other guy."

"Oh, okay." Jason looked around the little room. "So, you want to watch TV?

"No. I don't want to do anything with you."

Jason shrugged. "That's no sweat off my back."

Jason moved back to the couch and flipped on the TV. After scrolling through the channels he turned it off again.

"Aren't you bored?" he asked looking over at the boy who sat cross-legged on the bed.

"No," Zach answered.

"How old are you anyway?"

"I don't have to tell you anything."

"I'd say you're about five." Jason guessed low and it had

the desired effect.

"I am not." Zach clambered out of the bed and stood tall. "I am six and a half."

"Oh, I can see that now that you're standing up like a man and not crying all over the place."

"Sometimes you have to cry," Zach told him seriously moving closer. "My Mom told me that when Daddy was crying."

"Why was he crying?"

"'Cause you were trying to take his store."

"I'm not taking his store. I just work for the people who want it."

"Why do you work for them?" Zach leaned on the arm of the couch.

"It's just like your dad. If I don't people will get hurt."

"You will get hurt?" Zach asked curiously.

Jason shook his head. "No, they can't hurt me."

"So why do you do it?"

Jason patted the couch beside him and the boy climbed up. "Sometimes when someone is trying to do what is right, he has to get close to what is bad to stop it."

"So you are helping my Daddy?" Zach looked up at him hopefully.

Jason looked away. Why had he even gone there? Now this kid could ruin the whole operation just when he was getting somewhere. "It's kind of hard to explain."

"So you are not a bad guy, you are just pretending to be one like they do in the movies?"

Jason glanced at the closed door hoping no one was listening in. "Listen, Kid. You can't tell anyone…" Jason paused then started again. "You know how in the movies if someone tells the bad guys that the good guy is just pretending to be bad, then the good guy gets in trouble?"

"Yeah."

"So you have to keep it a secret or you will blow my cover and the bad guys will win. Even if you are very scared or very mad you cannot tell."

Zach nodded seriously. "I am very good at keeping secrets."

"I hope so," Jason told him.

Zach leaned against Jason and sighed. "Do you think you will beat them before they hurt my daddy again?"

Jason looked down at the little boy and ruffled his blond hair. "I'll do the best I can."

FOURTEEN

"How'd it go?" Benjamin asked.

Jason shut and locked the door. "Great, he's a nice kid."

Benjamin nodded. "I hope his dad is smart enough to let go of the store." He tossed his duffle bag onto the couch and looked at Zach who was playing quietly on the floor.

"What do you have there?" Benjamin asked.

Zach glanced at Jason before answering. "Mr. Cargo made me sock puppets."

"Mr. Cargo huh?" Benjamin grinned at Jason. "Nice."

Jason rolled his eyes. "He had to call me something other than 'bad man.'"

Zach came over to them still wearing one of the crudely made puppets. "Are you leaving?" He looked scared.

"Sure, remember I told you I have to go to work today."

"Can't he go for you?" the boy asked, pointing at Benjamin.

"I think the kid's attached to you, Cargo." Benjamin tried to smother his amusement.

Jason knelt in front of the boy and put his hands on his shoulders. "Listen, Zach, I have to go now, you be a brave boy and obey Mr...Scott. Alright?"

Zach nodded glancing at Benjamin.

Jason rose and went to the door "Good, I'll be back to see you sometime."

Zach's lip had begun to quiver, and he nodded again.

Jason left quickly, his heart broke for the poor kid. How

117

terrifying it must have been to be snatched out of his house in the dead of night and holed up somewhere with a bunch of thugs. Even if it blew his cover, Jason knew he had to get the kid out of there.

———

"Hey Roper."

Jason smiled politely at Officer Wayne, his smile faded for a moment as his eyes fell on the man beside the officer. He caught himself and smiled once more. The man with Wayne reminded Jason of Mr. Jarris. He had the same thin face, and though his gray hair was cut short and styled differently than Mr. Jarris' the resemblance was unmistakable.

"How can I help you, gentlemen?" Jason asked.

"Mr. Lario, I'd like to introduce you to Jason Roper, he's been working here for about two weeks now, isn't that right?" Wayne asked.

Jason nodded "Two weeks today."

"Jason, this is, Mr. Lario, chief of police."

"Good to meet you, sir." Jason had already guessed that was who he was, but he offered his hand and Lario shook it.

"I wanted to apologize to you for dragging you down to the station the other day," Wayne told him looking around the busy diner.

"No problem, you were just doing your job." Jason's mind was scrambling to connect the dots. Wayne was not a regular customer at the diner and Jason knew his introducing Lario was not just a coincidence. So this was the missing brother. Jarris and Lario were the infamous 'Jarris brothers' everyone was trying to stop. The 'cops day off' raids made sense now. It was a sweet set up to have one brother working as the gang leader, and the other as the police chief. No wonder the gang had done so well. If only he knew where his father fit in.

"I was wondering what tables you are serving today,"

Wayne said drawing Jason's thoughts back to the present.

"I'm on the booths on the right, under the windows," Jason answered pointing them out. "Or if you prefer an open table I've got the three closest to the counter there."

"We'll take a booth."

"A booth it is." Jason led the way to an empty booth near the back of his row. "Is this okay?"

Wayne looked at his guest who nodded. "This is fine."

Jason waited for them to be seated then handed each a menu.

"When did you get promoted to a waiter?" Wayne asked scanning the menu.

"This is my first day," Jason told him. "I'll still be a bus boy on the side though, same as the other servers."

"Is the pay any better?"

Jason shrugged, "I guess I'll find out on Friday. What can I get you gentlemen to drink?"

"I'll have a Dr. Pepper," Wayne told him, "Go easy on the ice."

Jason jotted it down and looked at Lario. He had the same evil glint in his eyes as Mr. Jarris. "I'll take a Coke."

Jason nodded. "I'll have that right out for you." He stopped at another table on his way to the kitchen, "Is there anything else I can get you?"

The ladies at the table smiled and shook their heads. "Everything was wonderful."

"Good." Jason pulled the little black tab book from his apron pocket and laid it on the table. "Whenever you are ready." He left them to finish and went to get the drinks.

"Looks like you are on better terms with those cops," Angie observed. She brushed a wavy strand of hair out of her face before she picked up the loaded tray from the counter.

"Whatever it was that Mr. Weaver told him seems to have set him straight," Jason answered. He scooped ice into the glasses and started filling them.

"Amy said they had you at the station on Saturday for questioning."

"Yeah, some guy with the same build as me was at the Taylor kidnapping. I almost didn't go to the movie theater that night but I'm glad I did. I don't think I could have proved I was home that night, because there wasn't anyone who would have seen me."

Angie nodded. "I just wish these gangsters would pick another town to ruin."

"Or get rounded up and put in the slammer," Jason replied putting the glasses onto a tray. He grabbed a few extra straws and shoved them into his apron.

"Wouldn't that be nice." Angie said sarcastically as she left the kitchen.

Jason followed her out. "It could happen."

"You're such an optimist, Jason," she told him splitting off to deliver the food she carried.

Jason set the glasses down and dropped the straws beside them. "Are you ready to order?"

"Is the Philly cheese burger any good?" Lario asked.

"I'm not partial to mushrooms myself," Jason responded. "But a lot of people order it, so I guess it's pretty good."

Lario folded the menu. "I guess I'll give it a try."

"How would you like it?"

"Medium rare."

"Alright…" Jason scribbled the order on his pad then looked at Wayne. "And for you?"

"I think I'll try your special." Wayne answered handing him the menu.

"Great, I'll have that right out to you."

———

"Jason Roper?"

Jason glanced at the car that had slowed beside him, but kept walking. He could not seem to place the voice he heard.

"Jason, get in." the door opened and Jason bent to see the driver.

"Mr. Taroe?" What was his father's chauffer doing way out here?

"Get in," Mr. Taroe repeated, his deep voice was commanding.

"I don't think so." Jason closed the door and kept walking.

The car sped ahead and parked on the curb. Jason considered turning around but decided against it. Taroe got out as Jason approached.

"I need to have a word with you, Jason."

"I go by Roper here," Jason told him folding his arms and raising his chin defiantly.

Taroe glanced around nonchalantly before speaking. "I'm not a chauffer, Roper. I am a federal agent. I was sent to investigate your father."

Jason waited for him to say more.

Instead, Taroe opened the car door. "Will you get in?"

Jason hesitated then shrugged. "I guess I'll chance it." He climbed in and Taroe shut the door behind him. Jason tried his door, it still opened from the inside. He pulled it closed as Taroe got into the driver's side. Taroe put the car in gear and pulled away from the curb.

"So let's see the badge." Jason was skeptical.

Taroe reached into the breast pocket of his suit coat and pulled out a black leather ID badge and flipped it open to show the official looking badge.

"Alright, I'm all ears."

"What do you know about your father?" Taroe asked.

"You tell me what you know," Jason replied. Had his father sent Taroe to feel out the situation? The badge could easily have been made by his father's men just like Jason's ID's were.

Taroe shook his head. "You are the most untrusting person I've ever met."

"Do you blame me?"

Taroe looked over at him for a moment, then shook his head. "No."

"Then let's hear it."

"Your father is heavily involved with the gang you are dealing with here. It is a small gang known as the "Jarris gang" or the 'Jarris brothers.'"

Jason waited.

"We have suspected your father was involved for some time now, which is where I came in. I, much like you, exchanged my name for a cover name and totally buried my records. I have been working undercover for your father for several months now and have already gathered enough evidence to keep him in prison for a long time."

Taroe fell silent, letting the information sink in as he drove toward the edge of town. "You're awfully quiet."

"How long has my father been involved with the Jarris brothers?"

"As far as I can see it's been about two years in the making."

"So, all the time he was training me, he was working as a crook on the side." Jason's jaw muscles worked as he tried to control the hot anger that rushed over him. "The two-sided skunk."

They rode in silence once more.

"He did it because of me didn't he?" Jason finally asked.

Taroe looked over at him. "What do you mean?"

"You don't know about 8/15?"

Taroe frowned. "I have heard McCard mention that only once."

"8/15 is a compound my father stumbled across when I was three years old," Jason told him. "He researched it, did a few tests on it, and then gave it to me. Like some lab rat."

Jason spat bitterly.

"What does it do?" Taroe asked pulling the car off onto a country road and parking in the deep shadows beneath some overhanging trees.

"It takes fifteen years to fully invade the body. Once that time is up, which happened on my 18th birthday, it kicks in and eight months and fifteen days after that the body is rendered indestructible."

"Meaning?" Taroe was having trouble grasping the concept.

"Meaning I could pull a gun out and point it at my head, pull the trigger and go on living as if nothing ever happened," Jason answered. "I don't feel any physical pain anymore."

"Wow," Taroe shook his head. "Will you always be that way?"

Jason ran his hand through his hair, a bad habit he was growing quite fond of. "That is something that is a little confusing since I really don't understand how it works."

Taroe thought about it then asked "So, do you mind being…painless?"

Jason shrugged and looked out the window. "My dad always said I was meant to be a hero, and to change the world. But now I see it was all a sham."

"It isn't a sham, Jason," Taroe told him. "If you really are invincible there is so much you can do for the world, so many people you can help."

"Yeah, that's what he said," Jason told him bitterly. "He could have just saved me the time and gone straight. You don't know what I've given up for this dream of his."

Taroe nodded in the growing darkness. "I know this is hard for you."

Jason sat up. "What about my mom, is she a part of all this?"

Taroe inhaled slowly and let it out. "Jason, your mom is dead."

Jason bit his lip and looked away slowly shaking his head. He pushed open his door and climbed out.

"Jason."

Jason paused.

"I want you to know your mother was not involved," Taroe told him gently. "She must have known about the 8/15 but she wasn't involved with the other things your father was doing."

"Did he kill her?" Jason asked without looking inside the car.

Taroe did not answer right away. "Not directly," he finally said when he saw Jason was not going to let it go.

Jason nodded and walked a little ways from the car. Taroe watched him in the side mirror. Jason stood for a moment and Taroe saw him swipe angrily at his eyes. Jason walked a little further from the car, then sat in the darkness, clutching his knees to his chest, tears streaming freely down his face.

Taroe waited as the moon came up silently over the still countryside shining brightly down on the lonesome figure sitting in the grass. Finally, Jason rose stiffly and returned to the car. Opening the door, he slid into the passenger seat. "I'm ready," he told Taroe. There was a fierce determination in his voice.

Fifteen

"Listen, there's a way for you to get the kid." Jason glanced around the store. It was almost closing time so there were not many people around.

On the other side of the rack, Officer Joe Mckilligin picked out a dress shirt and looked it over. "Where is he?"

"There's two conditions you have to agree to first," Jason told him without looking up from the rack he was going through.

"Let's hear them."

Another customer walked up and they fell silent as he browsed through the hanging clothes. Jason moved to another rack and Joe followed once the other man had gone.

"First, you have to let the guy watching him go. The kidnapper escaped capture, got it?"

"What is the other one?"

"You get the kid and his mother out of town to somewhere safe."

"And I never talked to you?" Joe asked holding up a pair of pants and looking at them in a pillar mirror a few feet away.

"That's a given," Jason answered when Joe returned.

A clerk walked up to Jason. "Five minutes till closing."

"Thank you," Jason answered. The clerk went on down the row and told Joe the same message.

"I'll let him go, and get the kid out of town, what's the plan?"

"You've got to get to the hotel, get someone who can stay there all day tomorrow, without being noticed. Dress him up as a custodian or something."

"What floor?"

"Sixth, room 602. The guy guarding him has to go out for groceries sometime that day. Give two sharp knocks and the kid will let you in. He will be gone ten minutes at the most so you've got to be right there."

Joe checked his watch and headed for the door, thanking the clerk on his way out.

Jason hung around a few more minutes then left the store and headed for the hotel.

———

"What are you doing here?" Benjamin asked sternly.

"I told the kid I'd come see him," Jason answered.

"Mr. Cargo!" Zach ran to him and threw his arms around him.

"Well, while you are here, I can run out and get some more food for the kid."

"I'm not staying that long," Jason told him. "Besides everything is closed already. Maybe I can come on Thursday."

"We are out of almost everything. I'll have to leave him alone to go for food." Benjamin's patience was obviously running thin. "I've been stuck with the kid for two days straight. He's about to drive me mad."

"I've been good as I could," Zach told Jason.

Jason smiled down at him. "I know you have, but you have to give Mr. Scott a break now and then."

"There's nothing to do here," Zach answered walking the length of the bed and running his hand over the wrinkled blankets. "I'm tired of watching TV."

"Maybe this will help." Jason pulled something wrapped in a plastic sack out of his jacket.

"You brought him a gift?" Benjamin looked skeptical. "Don't you think you are getting a bit attached?"

"Hey, I brought it for you as much as for him," Jason answered handing Zach the sack. "If he's entertained you don't have to do it."

Zach unwrapped the sack and examined the contents: a three pack of Hot Wheel cars and a folded plastic mat that was printed with roads and scenery for the cars to drive on.

"This is cool." Zach's eyes were bright with excitement. "Thanks, Mr. Cargo."

"Sure. Don't open them until tomorrow morning, that way you can play with them all day."

"Hey, I'm going to hop in the shower real quick while you are here. See if you can convince him to stay here when I'm out tomorrow. You seem to have a way with him." Benjamin grabbed his bag and went into the bathroom.

Jason made small talk with Zach until he heard the shower turn on, then he got serious. "Zach, someone is going to come and get you out tomorrow while …Scott is gone." Jason kept his voice low just in case Benjamin was not in the shower yet. "You can't let on that you know, but you got to be ready all day. Don't look ready, just be ready. He'll probably go out when you take a nap."

"I told him I'm too big for a nap," Zach responded.

"But he still makes you take one right?" Jason pressed.

"Yeah." Zach was not happy about it.

"Okay, listen, Zach. You've got to act normal. Play with the cars but don't be overly good. When he tells you it's time for a nap, fight it a bit like you normally would, but not too much." Jason could only hope it was all going in. "Then pretend to go to sleep fast. If you have to put your head under the covers do but don't really sleep or you'll miss the guy coming for you. He's going to knock two times, tap tap. Then you run let him in. Got it?"

Zach nodded but Jason was not sure he did.

"Just don't say anything about it or we won't be able to rescue you. We've only got one chance at this."

The shower turned off and Jason stuck Zach into the bed and pulled the covers up to his chin. "Don't sleep in too late and keep an ear open for the knock all day," Jason whispered.

The bathroom door opened and Benjamin came out.

"Sleep well, and try to behave for Mr. Scott tomorrow, okay?"

Zach nodded. "I'll try, the cars will help."

Jason grinned. "I hope they do." He stood and faced Benjamin and added in a low tone, "for your sake."

Benjamin went with him to the door.

"I don't know if he'll really stay or not," Jason told him quietly. "Maybe try when he is taking a nap just in case."

Benjamin nodded. "That's a good idea, he usually sleeps about an hour when I finally get him down. That would give me plenty of time to get what we need."

"Any sign that Taylor is giving in?"

"No," Benjamin glanced back toward the boy, "One of the guys came by yesterday and said we are giving him till Friday."

"What will happen to the kid then?" Jason knew they only had one chance at this, and his voice carried his concern.

Benjamin shrugged. "I don't know. Let's just hope Taylor gives in."

———

"You tipped them off didn't you?"

Jason started at the fierce tone and looked up to see Frank storming toward him. The scar on his face stood out white against his angry red face.

"Frank, I'm at work," Jason reminded him uncomfortably.

"I don't really care where you are," Frank bellowed. "You went too far this time."

"Jason, who is that?" Mr. Weaver asked from behind the counter.

"I'll take care of it." Jason moved quickly out of the diner; Frank was right on his heels. Jason spun on him. "What do you mean storming in there like that, and spouting personal business off to the world?"

Frank shoved Jason's chest, and Jason stepped back to catch his balance. "You've been gumming up the works since you stepped off that lousy bus. And I'm here to stop it here and now."

"Listen, you've got it all wrong..."

"No, you do." Frank went for his gun and Jason punched him hard. Frank's head snapped back and he stumbled from the impact. Jason stayed on him, folding him with another fist in his stomach. Grabbing Frank's gun, Jason shoved him to the ground. A crowd was forming around them murmuring with excitement.

Jason stood over Frank, holding the gun in both hands. "Someone call the cops."

Frank wiped his bloody nose with the back of his hand. "You'll pay for this, Roper."

"Keep quiet," Jason ordered keeping the gun trained on him. "You're through."

Officer Dustin Jeffries pushed his way through the crowd. "What's going on here?" he demanded.

"That thug attacked my employee and tried to draw on him, Officer," Mr. Weaver told him before Jason could answer.

For once Jason was glad his boss was outspoken.

"Get up." Dustin had his own gun out now.

Frank glared hatefully at him but slowly obeyed.

Another police car pulled up with lights flashing and they quickly assessed the situation. Dustin approached Jason who handed over Frank's gun without protest. Stepping aside, Jason let out his breath, still tense and ready in case Frank tried to make a move.

The cops snapped cuffs on Frank and fairly dragged him to the car. He struggled against them, all the while bellowing at Jason as if he were out of his mind.

Dustin shut the door, cutting off the stream of threats. Jason saw the officer sigh and knew he was grateful to finally have Frank in his custody.

"Do you mind coming down to the station to make a statement?"

Jason looked at Mr. Weaver. "Would that be alright?"

"The man just tried to kill you, Jason. Of course you have to give a statement."

Jason nodded and followed Dustin to the other police car that had just pulled up. Dustin walked to the passenger window. The window rolled down and Dustin leaned on the sill. "Hey Mckilligin, do you and Wayne mind giving us a ride down to the station? We just had an attempt on this man's life."

Joe opened the door and Dustin stepped back to let him out. "Not if you don't mind riding in the back."

Dustin grinned as Joe pulled the back door open. He climbed in and scooted to the far side.

"You coming, Roper?"

Jason climbed in and pulled the door closed.

"So who was that guy?" Dustin asked as the car pulled away from the curb.

"I just know him as Frank. I don't know his last name, but he's heavily involved with the gang."

"Was this over the kid escaping?" Wayne asked, glancing at him in the mirror.

"Yeah, he was pretty sore about it. How did that go?"

"It was smooth. The kid opened the door right when I

knocked and was all ready to go. He had his little matchbox cars tucked in his pockets and everything."

Jason smiled sadly. "Good, I'm glad he's okay."

"We had someone pick up Mrs. Taylor and we've got a man driving them to a safe house," Joe looked at his watch. "I'd say they are about a hundred miles out by now. We have a man assigned to Taylor."

"Oh," Wayne chipped in. "Taylor asked us to thank whoever tipped us off, I guess that's you."

Jason met his eye in the rearview mirror, grinning at the awkward way Taylor's thanks were delivered.

They pulled up to the station and waited while the officers forcibly guided Frank through the doors.

"Be careful what you say, Roper. Stick to the facts." Wayne opened his door. "Alright, let's get that statement."

Sixteen

"Benjamin." Jason ran to catch up. "How did you get out?"

"I wasn't in," Benjamin answered. There was a coolness in his voice.

"Man, I'm glad they didn't get you. I haven't seen you for weeks. When I heard they had got the kid I thought for sure they'd taken you in as well."

"Is that what you wanted?" Benjamin stopped walking and faced Jason head on.

Jason looked confused. "No, man, I just thought they had."

"You tipped them off."

Jason frowned. "Not you too?"

"You put Frank in didn't you?" Benjamin asked accusingly.

Jason pulled him out of the main street into an alley. "Benjamin, Frank came storming into the diner, and was spouting off in front of all the customers. I got him outside and he tried to draw on me. There was a whole crowd watching because he was making such a row about it."

"So you let the cops take him to get him off your hands."

Jason was getting mad. "What was I supposed to do, Benjamin? Say, 'Oh, actually this is a friend of mine. I know he's yelling about kidnapping that kid and all, but he's a good guy. He just wanted to pull the gun out to let me see it.' Come on, Benjamin. I mean really, what would you have done differently?"

Benjamin shrugged. "I don't know. If you hadn't squealed

in the first place…"

"They would have had you kill the kid," Jason told him bluntly. "I told them I don't do kids. That was taking it too far and you know it. So Taylor won't give Mr. Jarris fifty percent of the profits from his store. I wouldn't either."

"You've been working with the cops from day one," Benjamin spat angrily.

"What if I have? I saved your skin didn't I?"

"What do you mean by that?"

"I told them to let you go." Jason locked eyes with Benjamin. "That was one of the conditions for me squealing. Do you really think it's normal for a cop to wait until the kidnapper is out to do the raid and then not wait around for him to return?"

Benjamin did not answer.

Jason walked a few feet away, running his fingers through his hair in frustration.

"So, now what?" Benjamin asked, his tone hurtful. "Are you going full time for them?"

"I wasn't planning on it," Jason answered. "What the gang is doing is wrong, Benjamin. You know it, I know it. The whole world knows it."

"You got to make money somehow," Benjamin shot back. "I can slave away at some janitorial job and make next to nothing or I can join a few raids and be set for a month. It's really not a hard choice."

"But it's a choice you are going to have to make now," Jason told him seriously. "I lost everything including my best friend when I came out here, and I'm willing to do it again to stop Mr. Jarris from taking more lives."

Benjamin was silent.

"So, are you with me, or do I go on alone?"

"You're really serious about this aren't you?" Benjamin's voice had softened some.

Jason nodded. "Yeah, I am."

"If I don't join you, what happens?"

"I'll have to treat you like I would any other member of the gang," Jason replied.

"So, you'd shoot me?" Benjamin pressed.

Jason took a deep breath and let it out slowly before answering. "If you chose to stay with them, and it came to that, I would have no choice." He paused and met Benjamin's eyes. "But it would kill me to do it."

"What about that other friend, did you kill him?"

"No, I was on my way to come here. So, it never came to a head. As far as I know he could still be gunning for me."

"What's this?"

Jason spun to see Gary approaching them, gun in hand. His big form practically filled the little alley.

"You traitors planning your next move?"

"What do you want, Gary?" Benjamin asked angrily.

Jason stepped in front of Benjamin with his back to him.

"You stay out of this, Benjamin," Gary warned.

"I've been expecting you, Gary," Jason told him calmly. "I knew from day one we were going to have to have a showdown."

"You've gotten in the way long enough," Gary told him.

"What are you going to do about it?" Jason asked without fear.

"I'm going to give you ten seconds to clear out."

"Get out of here Benjamin." Jason's tone was urgent and Benjamin obeyed, sprinting out the backside of the alley.

Gary grinned, "One…"

"Listen Gary…"

"Two…you'd better start running."

Jason looked at him, unfazed.

"Three…"

Jason turned and walked out of the alley onto the main

street. "Listen up," Jason yelled. People all along the street stopped to listen. "There is a man with a gun in that alley. He's looking for blood. You need to get clear of this area."

A ripple of panic swept over the people and they started running.

Jason spotted Benjamin who was peering around the side of the post office.

"Gary, I'm not going to run," Jason called loudly. He unzipped his jacket and stood ready.

Gary stepped from the alley, his eyes cold with hate. "You aren't as smart as I thought."

"You pull that trigger and you are a dead man," Jason warned.

"At least I'll take you with me." Gary spat on the sidewalk.

"No," Jason corrected, "you'll go alone."

"We'll see about that." Gary raised the gun and squeezed the trigger. The bullet struck Jason in the chest.

Jason whipped out his gun and Gary's eyes grew big. "I..."

Jason's bullet found its mark and Gary was dead before he hit the ground.

Jason stood looking down at the body of the big man. A wave of nausea washed over him and cold sweat trickled down his back. For a moment, it seemed as if time had ceased. All he could see was the body, lying lifeless before him. The wail of sirens grew steadily nearer penetrating his thoughts and drawing him back into reality. Jason knew he could not have done anything to spare him, but somehow that did not seem to help.

"It's amazing he missed at that close of range," A man said, approaching timidly to look at the body.

Jason ignored him. He returned his gun to its holster, and partially zipped his jacket to conceal it. Just seeing it made him feel sick to the stomach.

Another man came over. Now that the danger was over the crowd was returning to gawk at the body on the ground.

"Can you believe he missed?" the first man asked the second.

"Son, you're lucky to be alive," an older gentleman told him gently.

Jason turned away, trying to steady his breathing. Someone made another comment but Jason did not hear it. He moved away from them, not bothering to look back. The cops would be there soon to take care of things. He had just taken a life. The thought weighed on him and he found his mind running through the whole thing again, offering different options he could have taken. Jason ran his hand across his face. He had taken care of two, possibly three depending on Benjamin's decision, of the gang members. Colby was pretty much out since Jason knew where to find him. That left him with Toby, Silas, Murphy, and the brothers. Jason leaned against the cool cement wall of the theater. People were spilling out of the theater and milling around out front, while the next wave of people pressed through to get in to the theater. Jason felt safe leaning there, lost in a crowd. He waited until the crowd thinned, then pushed himself off the wall and headed home.

A police car was sitting out in front of Mary's house when Jason arrived. He slipped into the neighbor's yard and hopped the fence, entering Mary's through the back door. The police were in the living room. Jason could hear them talking to Mary as he crept up the stairs. He paused at his door, instinctively moving to the side before pushing it open. A bullet tore through the silence and embedded itself in the flowered paper across the hall.

Jason heard the cops downstairs clambering into action. Jason pulled out his Glock and stepped into the doorway, training it on the man inside. He smiled patronizingly at

Murphy who stood braced in the center of the room. "That wasn't a smart thing to do."

"Neither was killing Gary," Murphy spat back.

They stood there tense and ready. Each waiting for the other to make a move.

"He's armed," Jason warned as the police started up the stairs.

The officers stopped where they were.

"Are you?" Wayne called up.

A little smile crept across Jason's face. "Yes, sir." His eyes were still locked on Murphy.

"You think you are going to get out of this. Don't you?" Murphy spat.

"Yeah, I do." Jason's gun twitched downward and Murphy's gun went off as he fell to the ground clutching his leg. Murphy pulled the trigger again and again as Jason rushed him, jerking the gun from his hands.

"Gary was right." Murphy clutched his leg, his eyes wide with terror.

Jason struck him with the butt of the gun and Murphy slumped to the floor unconscious.

"He's all yours, Wayne," Jason told them, tossing Murphy's gun onto the floor beside him. Once again he heard sirens in the distance; their backup was on the way.

Jason returned his gun to its holster and grabbed his backpack. He dug out the extra clips for his Glock and shoved them into his pocket.

"Where are you going?" Wayne asked.

Jason shrugged, "Wherever my feet take me."

"Roper, listen…" Wayne called and Jason paused at the top of the stairs. "You can't just keep doing this on your own.

"That's what I came here to do." Jason squeezed past Joe who was coming up the stairs and left the house without bothering to look back.

SEVENTEEN

Lario put down the phone and rose to pace his office. "McCard says he can do nothing to help."

"I told you that, didn't I?" Jarris stood by the door as if ready to run if he needed to.

"Yes, but what does that help? We've got some boy running around this city destroying what it has taken years to build up. Rumors are flying and my men are clearing out."

An urgent voice came over the radio on the desk and both men leaned in to listen. "Breaking news, the second captive left by the now infamous Jason Roper has been identified as Murphy Knight, a confirmed member of the Jarris gang. Authorities believe Roper is still gunning for the remaining members of the infamous Jarris Gang."

Jarris turned it off. "What are you planning to do about this, Bill?"

"What do you expect me to do?" Lario asked, resuming his pacing. "I'm in a bind. Our only chance is if your men can pick him off before he gets any further."

Jarris shook his head. "Is that the best you can do?"

"I can't put the police force after him now, Jarris. You heard the news, he's a hero. I have worked too hard for this position to jeopardize it now." Lario stopped to look at his brother. "You shouldn't have come here at all. If they find you here…"

Jarris rose. "If you and McCard think that I'm going to

take the rap alone, you've got another thing coming." His eyes gleamed with hate.

Lario's hand moved instinctively toward the gun on his desk but Jarris beat him to the draw. The gun barked and Lario fell against the desk, clutching his stomach. He reached for the gun but Jarris was ready. His gun barked again and Lario slumped to the floor, dead.

Jarris heard someone yell and the sound of several men running down the hall toward the office. He locked the office door, then picked up the phone and dialed. "McCard? Lario is dead." His tone was full of hate. "You'll be next if you don't stop Roper…you're the brains of this operation."

Someone tried the door. "Lario, are you okay?" His voice was muffled as he turned from the door, but Jarris caught the word key before someone ran off to follow his orders.

"I don't care how you do it," Jarris hissed into the phone. "Just get rid of him."

"Lario? Can you hear me?" The man pounded on the door. "Get someone around back, don't let anyone leave the station."

Jarris put the phone down gently and glanced around the spacious office. There wasn't time to destroy any evidence, but then he had no reason to. He had been the face for his older brother's schemes for long enough. Jarris made his way through a side door that led out to the back of the building, leaving Lario's cops to break down the door.

A lone man stood in the alley when Jarris emerged from the station. He was dressed all in black. His jacket hung open casually, but he stood firmly, his hands loose and ready at his sides.

Jarris froze, unable to explain the fear that crept into his heart at the sight of Roper.

"This is the end, Jarris," Jason told him firmly.

"You could kill me, but the gang would just move elsewhere," Jarris told him. "I'm not at the top of this thing."

"I know." Jason's gaze was steady and penetrating.

Jarris hesitated, and Jason saw his eyes dart to something behind him. He braced a little better, ready for any impact from behind.

He did not have to wait long. Something struck his head and Jason spun to see Silas behind him. In his hands he held the barrel of his gun.

"So you thought you could just pop me off." Jason jerked the gun out of his hand. Silas was too surprised to react.

"Gary was right." Silas had regained his composure. "That bullet at Taylor's really did hit you, didn't it?"

Jason did not answer him. "You have two choices. You can come easy, or we can do this the hard way."

"I don't think you are the one who should be giving us choices," Jarris told him. "You are badly outnumbered."

Jason reached for his gun but Jarris shot first. The bullet had no effect. Jarris shot again as Jason pulled out his gun and aimed it at Jarris. "Drop it."

Silas slammed into Jason, the impact knocking him off balance. He stumbled and Silas struck him again, knocking the gun from his extended hand. Jason had not expected Silas to be so strong. He moved toward the gun. Again the impact of Silas' fist drove Jason back. He felt no pain as he struck the brick wall. Jason struggled to right himself, to retaliate and stop Silas, but Silas had found his weakness. Roper was invincible, but he was not powerful. As long as he could keep pushing him, driving him back, the impact of his blows would keep him off balance and Jason would not be able to attack.

"So you thought you could just walk in…" Silas shoved him hard and Jason stumbled on a pile of bottles, "and destroy all we have worked for?"

Jason grabbed one of the bottles and hurled it at Silas,

who ducked out of the way. Jason threw another, scrambling to his feet with another bottle in each hand. The third bottle struck Silas and he stumbled back. Jason dove for the gun and turned it on him.

"Freeze!" Jason commanded.

Jarris had slipped away during the scuffle, leaving Silas to face Roper alone. Silas stood slowly.

"You don't think I have the guts?" Jason demanded.

"You don't, Roper. You will lose too much," Silas answered calmly.

Jason got to his feet. He knew Silas was buying time but he was curious to see how he would do it. "What do I have to lose?"

"You could have a great life. All you have to do is take out Jarris and you will have a ready made gang in your hands."

Jason laughed sarcastically. "Let me guess, you would work for me?"

"I can show you the ropes, get you connected," Silas offered. "Someone with your…gift would be unstoppable."

"I am," Jason told him. "Get against the wall."

Jason heard a commotion behind him. Seconds later several police officers burst out the back exit of the station. They brandished their weapons as they quickly scanned the street.

"Drop the gun," one commanded, training his gun on Jason. He was shorter than Jason by at least a foot. His thick neck and wide shoulders showed he was serious about keeping in shape for his job.

"This is the one you want," Jason responded, keeping his distance from Silas but not taking his eyes from him.

"Drop the gun," the officer barked. "We'll take care of you both."

"What is going on?" Jason demanded.

"As if you didn't know," the younger officer spat. "The

Chief was just murdered in his office. You gangsters are all the same."

Jason immediately recognized the rookie.

"Well, Bert Bently." Jason still did not take his attention from Silas. "Looks like you are hot on the trail. This isn't your man, but he'll need to be taken in for gang involvement."

"Who do you think you are?" the first officer demanded angrily.

"He's a reporter," Bently told him, trying to smooth things over.

The officer ignored him. "I said we'll take care of this. Drop your gun."

"Under normal circumstances I would comply," Jason told him.

"You'll comply now." He pointed the gun at Jason's head. "Drop it."

Silas moved slightly. "Don't think about it," Jason warned him darkly. "You aren't going anywhere."

"I'll count to three." The irate officer warned.

Jason was ticked. He turned on the officer. "You can count to a hundred if you want and nothing would change."

Silas made a break for it. He slammed into Jason pitching him forward and raced down the alley. Jason whipped around, his gun flashed once and Silas stumbled and fell.

"Don't move." The officer held the barrel of his gun just inches from Jason's head.

Jason complied.

"Get an ambulance out here," the officer ordered and Bently raced to obey.

Curious, Jason turned slowly so he could see the third officer who had stood silently through it all. His eyes widened and he quickly looked away.

"I'll cover him," the familiar voice sent a chill through Jason.

The officer nodded. "I'm not done with you," he told Jason angrily.

Jason waited, crouched on the cold ground as the officer stood over him.

"Your dad told me I'd find you here," Kirk said quietly. "But I wasn't expecting to find you so fast." Jason could not read any emotion in his voice.

Jason did not look up, not wanting Kirk to see the turmoil he felt inside. In silence, Jason watched the officer who stood over Silas. The ambulance came screaming down the road and Silas was loaded onto a stretcher.

The short officer strode back to where Jason waited. "You're lucky you didn't kill him."

"I wasn't trying," Jason answered in a low voice.

"I've had enough of your guff," the thick man told him. "I'm going to book you and let you cool off a bit."

Jason stood. "I'm sorry, but I have a previous engagement." He glanced at Kirk. What was he doing here, and in uniform? Jason wished he could talk to him, to find out what was going on behind his expressionless face. Kirk had been his friend. Somehow Jason had thought that he would not have to face Kirk again once he moved to another town. What he now knew told him there could be only one reason for his dad to send someone to find him.

The officer shoved Jason hard, pushing him up against the wall and attempting to pull his arm around behind him. Jason spun around and jerked his arm free. Shoving the officer away he scooped up his gun from the ground and ran. Behind him he heard a gun bark, but he did not stop.

He rounded the corner and barreled into Dustin. The officer instinctively stepped back, giving himself room to act.

"I'm sorry, Dustin." Jason glanced behind him.

"What's going on, Roper?" Dustin asked as the officer rounded the corner behind them.

"Jarris shot Lario and got away," Jason answered backing away.

"You dirty rotten…"

"Hold it, Margan," Dustin interrupted "This guy's helping us."

Margan looked confused but Jason could tell he was still mad.

"This is Roper, the guy on the news."

Jason glanced back to see Kirk standing at the corner, listening.

"He could have said something." Margan was not ready to let go of his pride.

"Jarris headed west down this street but I'm guessing that was almost ten minutes ago now."

"Jarris?"

"Yes, as in the Jarris brothers. I don't really have time to explain it all now."

"How can we help?" Dustin asked.

"I don't know, just let me do my job."

Eighteen

Jason turned and jogged down the street, racking his mind for where Jarris would hide out. He had been totally disconnected from the "big boss" and knew nothing about his hideouts or meeting places. He knew that is what Jarris had wanted, but he kicked himself for not investigating it better. He checked the office where he had first met Jarris, but the place was cleared out. Jason was aware he was being followed but he disregarded it, focusing on the task at hand. He went to the desk and pulled out the drawers one at a time. He found a scrap of paper in one but it was just an old receipt. There was nothing else in any of the other drawers. He looked around the room. Whoever had been on the cleanup crew had done a good job of it. He went out through the store to throw off his tail, but several blocks later he knew it had not worked. He turned a corner casually then flattened himself against the wall and waited. A few minutes later Benjamin walked by looking like he'd lost something.

"So you are tailing me," Jason said matter-of-factly.

Benjamin jumped. "I…"

"Was tailing you," Jason finished for him. "What do you want?"

"I've decided."

"Okay." Jason waited.

Benjamin glanced down the street and then met Jason's eye. "I'm with you, Roper, all the way."

Jason grinned and slapped him on the shoulder. "Welcome to the team."

"So now we are like a good gang?" Benjamin smiled weakly. It had been a hard choice for him and he knew it was going to get harder.

Jason shrugged. "I guess so."

"What do we do now?" Benjamin asked.

"I don't really know," Jason answered. The sun was setting fast and they were running out of time. "I don't know where Jarris would hide out."

Benjamin smiled. "I do."

Jason followed him down street after street until he had completely lost track of where they were. Finally, Benjamin stopped in front of a glamorous looking hotel.

"Wow, he really lives it up," Jason observed.

"Just follow me." Benjamin walked confidently through the automatic doors and up to the front desk. "Excuse me."

The clerk came over and Jason could tell right away the man was nervous. "What is it?"

"Is Mr. Jarris in?"

"No." The response was too fast.

"Good, I'll go right up." Benjamin turned and walked to the elevators, ignoring the clerk's weak protests.

Once they were in the elevator, Benjamin let down his guard. "Was that good or what?"

"You handled him like a pro," Jason told him with a grin. "We make a real team."

For a moment Benjamin was silent, as if soaking in the approval. He laughed, shrugging it off. "I guess we do."

The elevator beeped and they both looked up at the number. This was not the floor Benjamin had selected.

"This is it." Benjamin told him, seriously. "Showdown time."

"Let me go first." Jason moved forward as the doors slid

open. An oval shaped object arched toward him as he stepped into the hall, and he instinctively caught it. He looked down at the olive colored object lying in his hand. Suddenly it registered that he was holding a live grenade.

For a split second his eyes met Benjamin's. He could almost taste the fear as Benjamin groped for the elevator button. Jason sprinted away from the elevator. Dropping to the ground in fetal position he held the grenade close to his chest. Seconds later the grenade exploded. The impact stunned Jason. His body was flung into the air and collided heavily with the ceiling. Jason fell hard on the tattered carpet, broken glass and plaster showering down around him. He stood shakily, and looked around at the damage. Checking himself, he felt nothing and wondered if he was in shock. The impact itself had been emotionally draining and his clothes were torn here and there from the force of the explosion. Jason felt lightheaded and steadied himself against what was left of the interior wall. Looking down the hall he saw no sign of his attacker.

He remembered Benjamin and moved to the elevator. Its door was dented in but it was closed. Jason banged on it. "Benjamin? Are you in there?"

"Roper." Benjamin burst out of the stairwell. "You're alive."

"How did you…?" Jason pointed lamely to the damaged elevator.

"I hit the button for another floor and the door just barely closed before the explosion." Benjamin told him. "It shook the elevator pretty bad and I was sure it was going to bust and fall down the shaft."

Jason let go of the wall as the effects from the blast diminished.

"The police are coming," Benjamin observed hearing the sirens.

Jason nodded absently. "Who in their right mind carries

grenades?"

"I don't know. I've never heard of Jarris using them."

Their brown eyes met and Jason knew. "Kirk."

"Who's Kirk?" Benjamin asked when he saw the anger that swept through Jason.

"A traitor." Jason spoke through clenched teeth. "You'll be in danger if you stay with me. Get out of here. I'll meet up with you later."

"I can help you, Roper," Benjamin objected.

"No. This is an old fight I've got to finish. Kirk wants revenge, and as my friend you will become a handicap to me. I'm sorry, Jarris will have to wait."

"What if he skips town?"

"I'll skip after him." Jason's tone was hard. He sorted through the debris with his foot looking for his gun. When he found it, twisted and scarred from the explosion, he dropped it back into the rubble, exhaling in irritation. It would not be any help to him now.

"Take mine." Benjamin offered pulling his gun out.

"No. You need it more than I do."

"I've got another one." Benjamin grinned gently patted his belt line. "Never go without."

"Alright." Jason took the gun and shoved it into his waistband. "You can watch for Jarris if you want, but don't get shot."

Benjamin smiled a crooked little smile. "I know how to take care of myself."

Jason nodded distractedly. "I know." He met Benjamin's eyes and held out his hand. "Thanks."

Benjamin shook it, firmly clapping him on the shoulder with his free hand. "Be careful."

Jason turned and strode down the long hall. He took the stairs to the second floor and made his way to the more decorative carpeted steps that led to the lobby. People were flowing out of the building, crowding and jumbling together as they hurried toward the exit. Jason had never understood why people called for an evacuation after the damage was done. It made the perfect escape for Kirk.

Jason paused at the top of the lobby stairs, ignoring the people who jostled by him. The high ceiling gave him a nice view of the central area. He scanned the crowds. There were officers directing the flow of people all through the lobby. He had only caught a glimpse of the man who threw the grenade but he was sure now it had been Kirk. He struggled to remember if Kirk had still been dressed as a police officer, but he could only picture the grenade flying toward him. Something off to his right caught his eye. Jason turned slowly. There, across the big room, stood Kirk. His eyes darted down to something he held and Jason dropped his gaze to the grenade Kirk was holding.

Kirk's mouth twisted up in a hateful smile as their eyes met once more. Frowning threateningly, Jason shook his head slightly. He understood what Kirk was suggesting. The people were evacuating quickly and Jason knew if he could delay Kirk enough, they could make it out without being hurt.

Kirk gestured at Jason with a slight lift of his head then jerked his head toward the door. His meaning was clear, Jason was to come with him or a second grenade would be thrown among the fleeing people. He hesitated and saw Kirk slip his finger into the ring of the grenade pin.

Jason nodded once and started down the stairs keeping Kirk in his peripheral vision. When he was a few feet away, Kirk jerked his head toward the door again, but Jason stood his ground.

"I'll follow you," he told him over the noise of the people. Jason moved out of the flow into the little sitting area where Kirk stood.

Kirk cocked his eyebrow, unimpressed.

"You have my word," Jason told him.

"Put your gun on that table." Kirk pointed to a little table against the wall.

Jason laughed, but it was mirthless. "I wasn't born yesterday, Kirk. I'll put down my gun if you set down your grenade."

"You are a hero, Patrick," Kirk sneered. "You have to protect these people. But I have no reason to obey you. I will lose nothing if this grenade explodes."

"Except your life."

"What's that to me?" Kirk asked.

"You will be taking a lot of innocent lives, Kirk." Jason was having trouble understanding where Kirk was coming from. "It won't hurt me, and I'm the one you came to kill."

Kirk smiled patronizingly. "You are so naïve."

"How so?" Jason glanced toward the door. The crowd was beginning to thin out.

"You think you are buying them time," Kirk scoffed. "You are such a good hero."

"If you aren't here for me, why are you here?" Jason was truly curious.

"I'm not here to kill you, Patrick. I'm here to destroy your life," Kirk told him, his eyes gleamed with hate. "You and all your sweet little hero skills. I have something for you."

Jason's guard was up. "Which is…?" he asked emotionlessly.

"I have your mother."

Jason laughed bitterly, "Wow, Kirk. You are really behind." He glared at his old friend. "My Mom's dead, Kirk. You waited too long for that line."

"You think she's dead," Kirk responded but Jason had seen a flicker of hesitation and knew he was bluffing.

"Kirk, this is really lame, you and I both know you don't have her so just drop it." Jason was deadly serious.

Kirk shrugged. "Your dad thought you didn't know."

"There's a lot he doesn't know." Jason's eyes were hard. "A year ago I would have fallen for that, but not now. He's nothing but a liar. He will never be anything else."

Kirk rolled his eyes. "Like I care? I'll level with you. I have prepared a room, where I am holding several hostages."

"Really." Jason still did not believe him.

"Hear me out." Kirk's green eyes were bright with a cruel anticipation. "In this room there are only two pieces of furniture. A chair and small table."

Jason gave an exasperated sigh, his eyes drifted to the door where a cop stood guard. The officer was watching them intently, his gun drawn. Jason caught his eye and shook his head slightly, warning him to keep his distance.

"You're not paying attention," Kirk growled pulling a gun out with his free hand. "Should I eliminate the distractions for you?"

Jason locked eyes with Kirk, his look hard. He held his gaze for a moment and then relaxed and shrugged it off. "I don't think it would help. Am I honestly supposed to be understanding you?"

"You will." Kirk pushed his gun back into its holster. "The hostages will be released without being hurt if you will sit in the chair."

"Kirk, I'm sure you are having a blast being so mysterious, but I really don't have time for this." Jason locked eyes with him. "Frankly, I think you are still bluffing. Lay it out straight or this interview is over."

"I don't think you are in a place to decide," Kirk reminded him. "I'm going to take as much of your time as I feel like."

"Everybody clear out, there's going to be another blast!" Jason bellowed sending the officers scrambling for the door. He turned back to Kirk. "There, now you can do whatever you like with that stupid grenade." Jason sat on the lobby couch and propped his feet up on the coffee table. "Okay, let's play twenty questions."

Kirk hesitated, unsure of how to react.

"Is the chair an electric chair?"

"No," Kirk answered "I'm not that dumb."

"That's good to hear." Jason leaned back and put his hands behind his head. "Is there something on the table?" He saw Kirk's face twitch and grinned. "Okay, there's something on the table....could it be a clock?"

"That's enough," Kirk told him firmly. "I'm running this thing."

"No, you lost your chance," Jason told him, sitting up. "So my dad spilled the beans about my 'weakness' to digital clocks. Big deal. It doesn't work every day." He saw confusion on Kirk's face. "Oh, he didn't tell you that did he? Didn't tell you it only works one day a year? And even then, I don't believe it is true. How could looking at a clock at a certain time on a certain day neutralize something in my blood? It isn't logical, Kirk." Jason paused before adding in a gentler tone. "It looks like you got the same phony pitch I did. You don't have any hostages, Kirk. You're just blowing hot air."

Kirk opened his mouth to answer, but Jason cut him off.

"You can't hurt me, Kirk. You can try, you can threaten or attack, but you can't hurt me." Jason stood abruptly and snatched the grenade out of Kirk's hand. "I have nothing else to lose."

Kirk looked down at the pin that was still on his finger. Their eyes locked and Jason's look was cold. "You had better run, Kirk."

Kirk ran. He stumbled over a chair and scrambled to his feet glancing fearfully behind him as he raced for the door.

Jason's first impulse was to fling the grenade after Kirk. Instead, he turned away and hurled the grenade at a large decorative vase. It shattered beautifully, the shards reflecting the many lights of the hotel as they rained down onto the polished wood floor. Jason turned and left it there, as a symbol of the friendship that had once united them. His pace accelerated as the blast from the explosion pushed him toward the shattering glass doors.

NINETEEN

Benjamin watched as the police came pouring out of the hotel. They cleared the street, then gathered a few doors down on the other side to wait, milling around uneasily as they discussed their options. Benjamin stayed where he was, his eyes drifting back to the entrance of the hotel. After several minutes, he was rewarded with more action. A man ran from the hotel. He was about the same build as Roper but was wearing a police uniform. Benjamin pulled out his gun. A second explosion shot glass and debris out onto the street. Dust billowed through the broken doors.

Benjamin knew this young officer was his man. The officer was headed his way, glancing behind him at the damaged hotel. Even from a distance Benjamin could tell he was seething with anger. He waited, allowing the stranger to close the gap between them. As Kirk neared the corner, Benjamin stepped out in front of him.

"Hold on."

Kirk reached for his gun but Benjamin jabbed him in the chest with his own weapon.

"I wouldn't try it if I were you." Benjamin's voice was calm.

"What do you want?" Kirk demanded lifting his hands a little.

"Are you Kirk?" Benjamin asked.

"What if I am?" Kirk asked. "What business is it of yours?"

Benjamin nodded past his captive and Kirk turned to look.

Out of the dust walked a lone figure, he walked confidently his eyes scanning the street.

"So you're the bomber," Benjamin observed. "I guess those cops would like a word with you." He jabbed Kirk again. "Walk."

Kirk complied begrudgingly. He had gone the length of the building when suddenly he turned, knocking Benjamin's gun away from himself and drawing his own weapon. He pointed it in Benjamin's face. "Alright smart guy…"

"Drop it, Kirk." Jason's voice was firm and commanding as he crossed the street angling toward them.

"Not a chance." Kirk touched the barrel to Benjamin's head.

"Drop!" Jason shouted. His gun barked and Kirk jerked as the bullet entered his chest.

Benjamin dodged, knocking Kirk's gun barrel upward. Kirk pulled the trigger as he crumpled to the ground but the bullet only grazed Benjamin's hairline on its way past him.

Jason arrived at the scene at the same time as the police. Wayne knelt and took Kirk's pulse then shook his head.

"He's gone."

"Who was he?" another officer asked, still holding his gun as if unsure of who was the enemy.

"He's the man responsible for the blasts," Jason told them.

"Are you alright? You look like you were right in the middle of them," the officer responded.

"I don't know how you do it, Roper." Wayne rose still shaking his head. "You are always right in the middle of everything."

Jason didn't answer. He stood looking down at Kirk. He had known it would come to this but was not ready for the sorrow that enveloped him.

"You're Roper?" the first officer asked pushing his gun back into its holster.

Jason nodded without seeming to hear.

"Who's this?" the officer asked jerking his thumb at Benjamin.

Jason met the officer's eyes. "He's with me." His tone was hard.

The officer backed off a little. "That's fine."

Jason turned his attention to Benjamin. "Did you see Jarris come out?"

Blood trickled down from Benjamin's hairline and he shook his head slowly. "He never came out the front. But he could have used a back exit."

Jason took a deep breath and ran his fingers through his dirty hair, bits of plaster rained out as he did.

"Why don't you come down to the station and clean up a bit?" another officer asked kindly.

Jason hesitated then nodded. "Okay." The torrent of emotions that rushed through him was making it hard to think.

"I'll meet up with you later," Benjamin told him uncomfortably.

Nodding again, Jason followed the officers to their car and climbed in the back seat.

Jason leaned his head back on the headrest and closed his eyes, his breathing was shaky.

The officer shut the door and went to the driver's side.

"His things are in a backpack at Mary Page's house," Benjamin told him. "She can show you his room."

The officer passed on the information to his partner who jumped into the second car and took off toward Mary's.

"Thanks. That will mean a lot to him." The officer climbed in the driver's side. Benjamin shrugged in response.

Sirens announced the approaching ambulance that was coming to take away the body.

"Stick around and let them take care of that head wound. It doesn't look bad, but they will probably want to bandage it up," he called through the open car window.

Jason Roper

Benjamin watched as the police car carried Roper out of sight. Then he turned and strode off down the street.

Twenty

Jason sat silently, his head bowed and his fingers laced through his damp hair. The door opened, but Jason did not bother to look up. He heard someone enter but did not care. The bed squeaked as the visitor sat on it, then the room was silent again.

After several minutes, Jason slid his hands down across his face with a tired sigh and looked up to see Officer Mckilligin sitting on the bed.

Jason leaned back in his chair, his face was drawn and his eyes red from lack of sleep.

"They told me you weren't doing well," Joe told him quietly.

Jason sighed again returning to his former position, his fingers poking through his dark hair.

"Have you tried to sleep?" Joe asked.

Jason nodded without looking up.

"Have you eaten anything?"

Jason shook his head miserably.

"Roper, you've got to pull yourself out of this. I know what you are feeling." Joe paused and Jason straightened to look at the officer. "I have felt the depression you are feeling. We plan a big raid, and prepare for months, but once it is over there is blankness, a lack of purpose that could drive a man mad if he let it."

"It's not just the letdown." Jason's tired eyes met Mckilligin's. "I shot my best friend. I can deal with Gary. Sure

161

I had trouble sleeping after I killed him but he was an evil man and I was helping save lives. When I shot Kirk it was different. He was my friend and I was the one who pulled the trigger and ended his life." Jason looked at his hands. "I should have shot lower."

"You saved the life Kirk was trying to take, Roper. If you hadn't killed him he would have shot Benjamin and probably taken out a few cops as well. You did the right thing."

"I know that in my head," Jason answered softly. "But when I saw him lying there, his face…" He ran his fingers through his disheveled hair. "I just can't shake it."

Joe nodded but did not speak right away. "I know what you mean. There was a teenager who was gunning people down on the street a while back…I'll never forget his face."

"What do you do about it?" Jason really wanted to know.

"I pray," Joe told him.

Jason looked away.

"I know what you are thinking," Joe continued gently. "Religion is not going to help. Am I right?"

Jason gave a little shrug. He really did not care.

"Jason, you know how you went into that hotel and covered that grenade for Benjamin?"

"You and him are getting pretty chummy, huh?" Jason wished Mckilligin would leave.

"We did talk," Joe replied in the same calm tone. "The point is you took it for him not knowing if you would survive but knowing he wouldn't."

Jason nodded. The look of pure fear in Benjamin's eyes still haunted him.

"That's what Jesus did for you."

"They didn't have grenades back then," Jason reminded him standing slowly. He felt horribly weak and placed his hand on the dresser to steady himself.

"What do you need?" Joe was suddenly at his side.

Jason slumped back into the chair wearily. "I was…" Jason shook his head. "Never mind."

"I'll get it for you." Joe stood there waiting.

Jason shook his head again. "Its fine, go on." He knew Joe would not need a lot of prompting.

"Where was I?" Mckilligin asked sitting on the bed again.

Jason knew the officer was just trying to learn how much he had heard. "Jesus took the grenade for me," Jason told him without enthusiasm.

"Right." Jason could tell without looking that Joe was smiling. "You, like everyone else, were stuck between a rock and a hard place. Our sin had us backed up against the wall and in our hand was a live grenade. You and I were helpless, just like Benjamin was. No one else could have done what you did for Benjamin."

Jason waited.

"Jesus is the only one who can handle the grenade for us, Roper." Mckilligin continued. "He came and took that grenade, letting us go free." He paused before asking "What would you have done if Benjamin hadn't let you take it?"

Jason looked at him with a confused frown. "What do you mean?"

"What if Benjamin had taken the grenade from you and said he could handle it himself."

Jason looked away. "He would have died."

"That would have been pretty stupid, since he knew he had no chance of surviving the blast."

Joe got up and poured Jason a glass of water, before taking his seat once more.

"Yeah." Jason took it gratefully and drank.

"That's what you're doing, Roper."

The statement caught him off guard and Jason choked on the water. He held the glass out to Joe, coughing as he tried to clear his windpipe. "You did that on purpose didn't you?" He whispered hoarsely between coughing fits.

Grinning, Joe denied it.

Jason slouched down leaning his head against the back of the chair.

"Are you okay?" Joe asked putting the glass back on the little bedside table.

"Sure, I just do that for exercise," Jason croaked.

Joe laughed.

Jason glanced at him without moving. For a police officer, he had a good laugh. "What did you mean when you said I was being stupid?"

"You are hanging on to the grenade. Jesus has paid the price, He has conquered sin and death, but you just keep clinging to it. Roper you don't know when that grenade is going to blow, but once it does, it will be too late to give it up."

Jason did not answer.

"He can take it for you, it won't hurt Him at all. He's already suffered for your sin, it is paid for. All you have to do is give it to Him."

"You were referencing a grenade, but now "it" seems to mean something else," Jason observed.

"It's your life I'm talking about," McKilligin answered. "As long as you are running things, you are all there is to keep you going. Once you hit a low there is no one to pull you back up to the level ground. You've lost everyone you cared about…"

"My life seems to be pretty open to you." Jason sat up and glared at him.

"A federal agent came by last night to let you know that Nathan McCard had been arrested. He said you would want to know."

"So then he had to throw on an extra tidbit about my family?" Jason asked angrily.

Joe met his accusing eyes. "Roper, maybe he did talk too

much, but it helped me understand where you are coming from."

"Not that you needed to know," Jason told him looking away. "And don't go telling me you understand because all your family died too, 'cause I won't buy it."

"You think I'm lying to you?" Joe asked rising to his feet.

Jason looked up at him. The officer was tall and fit, his uniform was neatly pressed, everything about him showed he had it together. Jason knew Mckilligin did not have to be there. There was no ordinance saying officers had to cheer up depressed people that came through the station. Jason looked away. "No."

Joe nodded slowly. "I can see you've had enough of me. I won't overstay my welcome."

"Joe, I'm sorry." Jason sighed heavily. "I guess I'm still a bit sore about it all."

"That's understandable." Mckilligin placed his police hat on his head.

Suddenly Jason needed Mckilligin there. He needed someone to talk to. He stood, trying hard to think of a reason for the officer to stay.

Joe saw the desperation in his eyes. "Is there something I can get you?" he watched as the broken young man's eyes darted around for something to need, and smiled sadly. "Are you up to some food?"

"Yes." Jason felt stupid, why couldn't he just pull himself together?

"I'll get you something." Joe left the room.

Jason looked out the window. He had fallen along way from the cocky superhero he had been just a few weeks ago. Now he was broken, living on the hospitality of the officers he had helped. They were shelling out the rent for the hotel room he was staying in from their measly paychecks while he sat brooding about the past. He had lost count of the sleepless nights he had spent staring up at the ceiling. Down below he spotted a lone figure leaning against a building across the street. Even though he could not see him well, Jason knew it was Benjamin. He stood quietly, now and then Jason saw him glance up and down the street as if watching for someone. Only once did Benjamin's eyes drift momentarily up to Jason's window.

What if Mckilligin was right, what if his life ended and he was not ready. Jason moved away from the window and sat on the floor by the bed, his knees sticking up in front of him. He had often envisioned what would have happened if Benjamin had been caught in the blast, he had felt the sorrow of it in terrible nightmares. Jason wondered if that was how Jesus felt about him. If Jesus really cared about him half as much as people said, did it break His heart to think of Jason dying without His salvation? Jason had never thought of it like that before. He frowned, thinking hard.

Could it be true? His mom had believed in Jesus, Jason remembered her telling him and Kirk about God's love. As a kid, he had been more interested in other things and never really thought much about it. His dad, on the other hand, always brushed it off and reminded Jason to stay focused on the mission.

"You alright?" Joe asked.

Jason started.

"Sorry, I didn't mean to scare you." Joe shifted the tray of food he held. "Do you want it down there or at the table?"

"I guess here, since I'm already down here."

Joe set it down on the floor beside Jason. "You're getting to be quite the couch potato." He was rewarded with a little tired smile.

To Jason's surprise the officer sat down on the floor, leaning his back against the wall across from Jason.

"I was thinking."

"Eat while you talk," Joe told him, gesturing to the tray.

Jason rolled his eyes and picked up a sandwich.

"Okay, go on."

"This is your day off isn't it?"

"Yep, I got off about an hour ago," Joe answered. He removed his hat and looked questioningly at Jason. "Is that really what you were thinking about?"

Jason shrugged. "Sort of."

"Well, let's have the rest of it."

Jason took a bite of the sandwich to give himself time to formulate his answer. Joe polished the silver emblem on his hat with his sleeve while he waited.

"I was thinking about what you said." Jason expected the officer's eyes to light up with pleasure but Joe didn't even look up.

"What did you think?" he breathed on the emblem and gave it one more swipe with his sleeve.

Jason hesitated. "I think I understand what you were saying."

Joe nodded. "Good." He placed his hat on his knee and met Jason's eyes. "What are you going to do about it?"

Jason looked down at his sandwich. When he glanced up Joe was still watching him. "What do you want me to say?" Jason asked.

He shrugged. "You are free to say whatever you want."

"So this is like choose whose team you are going to be on?" Jason asked defensively.

Joe nodded thoughtfully. "I guess you could put it that way. You don't know if God will give you tomorrow, so it would be wise to choose today. You don't want to hold on to that grenade longer than you have to."

Jason put the sandwich back onto the tray and stuck his fingers through his hair, his elbows resting on his knees. He thought of Benjamin out in the alley guarding the street.

"How long has Benjamin been out there?" Jason finally asked.

Joe let him change the subject without objecting. "Since Wayne moved you here, which was three days ago now."

"He's been out there all that time?" Jason got to his feet and went to the window. "He just stays there?"

"When someone does something big for you, like you did for Benjamin, you feel a certain obligation to them. There is a bond between two people who have been so close to death together."

"You're talking about Jesus again." Jason raised an eyebrow at the officer who smiled back.

"You made the connection, not me," Joe told him crossing his long legs in front of him.

"So if I give my 'grenade' to God, there will be a 'bond' and I will want to serve Him?"

Mckilligin grinned. "You got it."

"So now what?"

"Now you think about it," Joe told him. "You have to decide if you want to give your life to Him and have that bond of service or if you want to keep walking around with that live grenade in your hands."

Jason looked out the window for a long time before nodding slowly. He turned back to Mckilligin with a determined look. "I'm ready to give it up."

Joe smiled and nodded. "Now all you have to do is let Him know." He pointed up past the ceiling.

"Do I have to get on my knees?"

"You're talking to the King of kings, but no, you don't have to kneel."

Jason moved to his knees and looked at Mckilligin who had not moved. "Aren't you going to do something?"

"No, this is between you and Him," the officer answered. "Just tell Him you believe His sacrifice was sufficient, and what you are going to do about it."

"Okay." Jason turned back to the bed feeling a bit awkward but knowing this was something he needed to do now. "Um…Jesus…I know You took the heat for me and everything and I believe that You are the only way for me to get to heaven. Uh… I want to give You my life." Jason relaxed and let the words flow. "The truth is I screwed it up pretty bad. I don't know what I'm supposed to be doing with this whole invincible stuff, but I figure You can use it somehow. I'm ready to work for You now, Jesus, to serve You instead of myself. I'm not going to hold on to this old grenade anymore, I don't think I'll make a real good Christian like Mckilligin is, but I'll sure try to do what You say. Thanks for dying for me." Jason rose and looked at Mckilligin. The officer's eyes shone with joy.

"What do I do now?"

"You do what He tells you," Joe told him getting to his feet.

Jason nodded, seriously taking the little black book Joe offered him. The words Holy Bible were inscribed in gold lettering on the front cover.

"I figured you'd need a travel size Bible." Mckilligin smiled and shook Jason's hand firmly. "Welcome to the family."

TWENTY-ONE

"Hi, Roper." Benjamin stuck his hand out awkwardly. "Good to see you again."

Jason felt just as awkward as he shook it. "Thanks for watching out for me."

Benjamin shrugged it off.

"Your head doesn't look bad."

Benjamin self-consciously touched the wound that started about half an inch from his hairline and disappeared into his thick brown hair. "Yeah, it's getting better. I didn't know you knew I got shot."

"I saw it happen, Benjamin," Jason reminded him.

"Yeah, but you were kind of out of it." Out of habit Benjamin looked up and down the street. "So, what's next?"

"Jarris is still out there." Jason told him. "It's my job to bring him in."

Benjamin grinned. "I was afraid for a while there that you weren't going to finish this thing."

"I wasn't," Jason told him truthfully. "But things are different now, and I'm ready."

Benjamin looked a little confused. "Okay."

"Have you had any leads on him?"

"Jarris? Yeah, he's hiding out here in the city. I guess he's waiting for orders." Benjamin's tone became excited. "Did they tell you about the whole gang thing?"

"I'm not sure."

"Apparently there was some bigwig way up who was running this whole thing. I don't remember his name, Poker or something to do with cards. Anyway, he was controlling both Jarris and Lario who was the chief of police. Plus, the police are keeping the fact that the big guy got arrested under their hats so Jarris is most likely hiding out waiting for instructions from him."

"Wow." Jason tried to sound surprised.

Benjamin's excitement faded. "You knew that didn't you."

Jason grinned. "Okay, I did. But you had fun telling it."

"See if I ever tell you anything." Benjamin shoved him. "Get lost."

Jason laughed putting a hand out to catch himself on the brick wall.

"It's good to have you back," Benjamin told him. He put out his fist and Jason bumped it with his own.

"Let's get to work."

———

Jason pushed the door open slowly. The room was dark inside. "Wait here, he may be armed," he whispered to the officer behind him. He moved into the room and closed the door behind him, waiting for his eyes to adjust to the dimness. The curtains were pulled shut and he could just make out the bed against the wall to his right.

"Colby?"

There was no answer.

"The cops are waiting outside, Colby. They know you're in here."

Still no answer. Jason reached to flip the light switch and was rewarded by a blast from the corner. He jerked his hand away instinctively.

"Colby, come on. It will be easier if you just come quietly."

"You traitor." Colby's voice was hard.

"Yeah, there seems to be a lot of those around here," Jason agreed softly.

"Is this why you saved me?" Colby asked bitterly. "To hand me over to the cops?"

Jason moved toward him in the dark. "No, I fixed your leg because I was trained to do that."

"Stay where you are," Colby commanded. Jason could see him now, he was seated in the chair close to the window. Jason could tell by the slight movement of the curtains that the window was open behind them.

"Listen, they have an ambulance out there, they'll take care of your leg…"

"Then throw me into prison?" Colby scoffed. "No thanks."

"You chose that when you started with Jarris, Colby. What did you think would happen?"

"I said stay where you are." Colby was pointing the gun at him with both hands, and Jason could see him trembling.

Jason reached out slowly and pulled the curtains open.

"I'm warning you, Roper." Beads of sweat were forming on Colby's brow and his eyes were glazed with fever. "I'm not going down without a fight."

Jason shut the open window and then held out his hand. "Give it to me."

Colby's trembling increased but he refused to give in.

Jason moved toward him. "Where's Toby?"

Colby sneered, "Like I would tell you, Traitor." He lowered the gun and squeezed the trigger, the bullet struck Jason's leg.

"It's no use, Colby." Jason put his hand around the barrel and pulled the gun out of Colby's weak grasp. "It's over."

"Gary was right." Colby's voice was tired.

"Yeah, he was." Jason gently pushed Colby back so he could rest against the chair. "Officer, you can come in. Bring the paramedics, he's in pretty bad shape."

The door opened, and Wayne and Mckilligin entered

hesitantly.

"He's here." Jason stood beside Colby, a hand on his shoulder to support him. "His fever is pretty high, we need to get him some help as quickly as possible."

"They are bringing the stretcher now," Wayne informed him taking the gun Jason offered.

The door opened and paramedics flooded the room. The officers stepped back to let them work, and Jason slipped out of the room.

———

"Toby is still at large," Wayne told the men around the conference table. "None of my men have seen any trace of him for nearly a month."

"Any ideas, Benjamin?" Jason asked.

Benjamin shifted uncomfortably in the big leather chair and shrugged.

"There must be somewhere he would go?" Wayne pressed.

"We all had personal plans for what we would do if the cops…I mean you guys, got Mr. Jarris." Benjamin told them. "He could be anywhere."

Jason did not meet his eyes; Benjamin was lying, but he did not know why.

"I was told this was a brainstorm meeting, not an interrogation," Benjamin continued. They all could tell his patience was running out. Benjamin had been working with them nonstop for over a month and was getting tired of being ordered around by Wayne.

"There are punishments for aiding criminals," Wayne told him seriously.

Benjamin's jaw tightened and his eyes narrowed. "I gave you the information to capture all of the other gang members, half of which you didn't even know existed. But if one gets away it's somehow my fault?" He stood abruptly. "I've had enough. Find someone else to push around."

"Sit down." Wayne was frustrated with the long delay.

Benjamin hesitated, his face expressionless, then walked toward the door.

"We are not finished here." Wayne folded his arms threateningly.

"Wayne." Joe's voice was firm but quiet.

Benjamin let the door swing closed behind him as he left the room.

"You're going to let this little punk go walking out on us like he rules the world?" Wayne's face was turning red and his voice was a little too loud, but Joe did not answer him. "Come on Joe. This kid is aiding and abetting a criminal, which is illegal. And you are siding with him?"

Joe looked away, but not because he was embarrassed for speaking up. He had made his point and silently held it.

"What are you trying to do, Joe? He's a gangster. For all I know he could have been the one that killed Clive."

Jason glanced between them uneasily, wishing there was a way for him to slip out of the room.

"You shot someone already for killing Clive, Wayne. You avenged him without knowing who his killer was." Joe's voice was still low and calm. "I don't think you want to repeat that mistake."

Wayne looked down, his breathing controlled and deep.

"Let it go, Wayne. This kid didn't do it. There wasn't anyone that young there and you know it."

"He may be shielding the one who did." Wayne slumped into one of the conference chairs. He rubbed his hands across his face. "I don't know, Joe. I just wish this was over with. The kid knows where one of the last members is and decides to hold out on us, drawing out the whole process. I'm fed up with the whole business." He looked up and frowned at Jason. "Why are you still here?" Wayne demanded.

"Um…" Jason had been sitting very still so he would not draw attention to himself. "I didn't know we had adjourned."

Wayne let out an exasperated sigh and waved him away. "Go find your friend. We're done." His voice was tired.

Jason obeyed, glad to be free from the stuffy room.

———

Jason found Benjamin sitting on the front step of Mary's. The little tabby was entwining herself around his legs, but Benjamin did not seem to notice.

"Hey." Jason sat down beside him and the tabby extended her circuit to include Jason's legs as well.

Benjamin grunted in response, toying with the tabby's tail as she passed.

"Is Toby going to start a new gang?"

"What, did they send you to pry it out of me?" Benjamin was irritated.

"No," Jason leaned back against the door. "Benjamin, I spent the last few months trying to clear up this gang. If Toby's just going to restart it all, I have to find him."

"And if he's not?" Benjamin pressed.

Jason shrugged. "I don't know."

"He's not like the others, Roper." Benjamin hesitated. "He's better."

"What do you mean?"

"Frank and Gary were cruel. They enjoyed hurting people, but Toby wasn't like that.'"

"But he helped them do it," Jason pointed out.

Benjamin rubbed the cat's ears. "Somehow it's not the same. Maybe he was like you, trying to stop it all."

"Can you look me in the eyes and tell me that?"

"I just can't rat on him. He was good to me, Roper. He helped me get started."

"With a gang."

"With life." Benjamin's voice rose. "He's a good guy, Roper. I'm not ratting on him so just drop it."

Jason fell silent watching a lone car make its way down the street. "Is he staying here, in the city?"

"Toby's off limits, Roper. I think I made that clear." Benjamin glared at him.

"Yeah, you made yourself real clear," Jason responded, trying hard to keep the irritation out of his voice. He brushed at the cat hair on his leg. "I'm just trying to figure out if I need to keep a lookout for him or if he's going to clear out of this area."

Benjamin relaxed a little. "He'll probably move on now that the gang is broken up."

They sat quietly for a while. Jason was grateful for the distraction of the tabby.

Jason glanced at Benjamin, and then broached a new subject. "Wayne thinks Toby killed Clive."

"Who's Clive?"

"I guess it was Wayne's partner, before Mckilligin."

"Frank killed him." Benjamin stated bluntly.

"How do you know?"

"He was always bragging about having killed a cop here because Jarris told them not to. He liked overstepping the rules and not getting caught."

"If Toby stays out of town, and you can convince Wayne that Frank killed Clive, that might get them off Toby's back." Jason told him

Benjamin shrugged.

"You'll still help us find Jarris though, right?" Jason asked dusting his pant legs again.

"Yeah, Jarris is nothing to me," Benjamin answered. "And I've got a good idea where he might be."

Twenty-Two

"Jarris. We've got the place surrounded, come out with your hands up." Wayne commanded. He was standing behind the squad car ready to duck if Jarris started shooting.

There was no response from inside the house. Jason looked around at the hoard of squad cars and officers that surrounded the little house. Beyond them, the countryside stretched out serenely for miles around. The huge trees swayed gently in the evening breeze, their branches brushing ominously against the house. They had been tracking Jarris for almost two months now, and had finally pinpointed his location. The house was small, unkempt, and looked like it had been vacant for years. A farmer who lived in the area had reported seeing lights shining dimly through the dirty glass of the windows.

"Jarris, this is your last warning," Wayne bellowed.

Still there was no response.

"Do you think he's in there?" an officer asked quietly.

No one answered him.

"Roper," Wayne called quietly, crouching behind the car.

"Sir?" Jason sprinted to his side.

"Do you want to bring him out?"

"Yes, Sir." Jason stood and looked at the house. He glanced at Mckilligin who crouched a few feet away. The officer gave him a thumbs up and Jason grinned. This is what he was born for.

Jason strode confidently to the door and knocked. A bullet tore through the wood and struck him. Checking to make sure the cops were covered, Jason knocked again.

———

Jarris waited, his eyes riveted on the door. A tendril of smoke rose from his gun barrel into the chilly air. The lights of the police cars flashed through the cracks in the dilapidated door onto the furniture around him. The furniture had long ago been covered with white sheets that were now moth eaten and supported a fine layer of dust. He heard two quick steps on the porch and braced himself. The door burst in, weathered wood flying in all directions in the little room. Jarris shot again his eyes narrowing, as the figure continued to move toward him. He watched the intruder, silhouetted against the bright lights of the squad cars.

"Roper." Jarris' voice was full of hatred.

A burst of flame in the dimming light announced the next bullet as it left the barrel.

Jason put his hand out. "Give me the gun."

Jason moved toward him. Again and again the gun went off. He wondered how long Jarris had been holed up in this dilapidated little house. The man who had looked so sharp on their first meeting was not the man that stood before him now. Jarris' face was covered in gray stubble and his clothes were dirty and wrinkled. Jason could tell the man was scared. Another bullet bounced off of him as Jason opened his coat and pulled out his gun.

"A month ago I would have shot you on sight," Jason told him. "But I've learned a lot since then." He took the clip out of his gun and laid the gun on the dusty table, slipping the clip into his pocket. "There is value in every life. Even yours."

Jarris laughed scornfully.

"You know this is pointless, Jarris," Jason told him firmly.

"Drop the gun."

"You think you've won, Roper," Jarris spat hatefully. "But you haven't even scraped the surface."

"Because you are not the mastermind behind all of your schemes?" Jason asked. "Would the name McCard mean anything to you?" Jason saw Jarris' eyes widen in surprise for a split second before he caught himself and the hateful look returned.

"Why should it?" Jarris asked glaring at Jason.

"McCard was captured, Jarris. The game's up."

Jarris' face did not change. "You are lying."

Jason shrugged. "I guess I can prove it when I take you in."

"You'll never take me in, Roper." Jarris backed toward a door that Jason guessed led to another room.

"Jarris, if you try to escape they will shoot you," Jason warned. "Come with me and you will be safe."

Jarris glowered at him. "Safe?"

"Yes. I promise that if you come with me, you will be taken safely to the police station."

"You liar." Jarris spat. He hurled the dusty mantle clock at Jason who easily dodged it.

Jason walked toward him. "Let's go."

Making a break for it, Jarris dodged through the doorway, slamming the door behind him. Jason tried the handle, it was locked. He heard Jarris scooting something heavy across the floor. Taking a few steps back, Jason moved forward quickly and slammed his shoulder into the door. It cracked loudly, Jason moved back and struck again. The third time the door broke and Jason pulled the pieces out of the way.

Jarris had moved a large dresser in front of the door. He stood across the room, his fear growing more evident as the dusky light faded around them. Outside the police turned on their spotlights and shone them on the house making the night around them seem darker.

Jason hopped over the dresser, and grabbed the older man firmly by the arm. Jarris jerked his arm away with surprising strength.

"I didn't want to do this the hard way," Jason told him firmly.

"There's isn't another way." Jarris' face was contorted with rage. "I won't give in." His voice held a note of desperation. He held up his fists like a prize fighter and moved toward Jason.

Jason shook his head. "You are wasting my time."

Jarris' fist connected soundly with Jason's jaw causing him to stumble back. The blows followed quickly driving Jason back. Jason ducked out of the way and pounced on him, shoving the gangster down against the bed. Jarris struggled against him and Jason leaned his weight against his captive. He twisted the gun out of Jarris' hand and tossed it through the window.

Jason pulled a pair of handcuffs out of the side pocket of his cargo pants. Snapping one onto Jarris' wrist, he rose and clicked the other handcuff onto his own wrist. "Let's go," he said, once again walking toward the door. Jarris fought him every step, jerking and pulling like an angry child.

Jason attempted to push the dresser out of the way but Jarris' jerking made it almost impossible. Jason stood and faced him.

"Jarris, I had respect for you when I met you. You were a big man with a lot of authority." Jason shoved him up against the wall, pressing the man's throat with his forearm. "I'd appreciate a little more manly behavior from you." Jason held him there a second longer as Jarris gasped for breath, then he moved away, pulling Jarris with him. Jarris complied, biding his time.

"Hold your fire," Jason called from the doorway. He heard Wayne repeat the command to his men.

"Alright, Roper. Bring him out," Wayne called.

Jason led Jarris, who was still seething with anger, across the yard to the waiting squad car. Joe released Jason from the handcuff. Jarris grabbed at the officer's gun with his free hand and Jason shoved him hard against the police car. He leaned in close, his eyes hard and full of wrath. "Don't try that again." His voice was low and threatening.

"Roper," Mckilligin warned.

Jason hesitated, and then let him go. He grabbed Jarris' arm and pulled it roughly behind his back, clicking the free handcuff onto his wrist. Jason shoved him into the car and slammed the door behind him.

"He's all yours," Jason told Mckilligin with a controlled calmness. He turned and strode away. Benjamin met him, grinning in the darkness. "You did great."

Jason angrily ran his fingers through his hair. "I lost it at the end. I told myself I wasn't going to do that."

"Roper, you brought him out alive." Benjamin watched as the squad car pulled out, its lights still illuminating the dark night. "I would have shot him."

Jason sighed. "I almost did."

"But you didn't," Benjamin answered. "Why?"

Sighing again, Jason looked back at the police who were packing up. "I gave my life to God."

Benjamin laughed heartily.

"I knew you would do that," Jason mumbled, turning to go.

Benjamin's laughter died and he laid a hand on Jason's arm. "Come on, Jason. I thought you were joking. I didn't mean…I just wasn't expecting that I guess," He finished lamely.

"It doesn't matter really," Jason told him. "What I did, I did for good."

"I'm not sure I know what you did," Benjamin replied hesitantly.

"I…" Jason met Benjamin's curious gaze. "I gave my life to God. I don't really know how to explain it. See, God sent

Jesus to take the punishment for my sin. Kind of like when I took that grenade for you. He paid for it with His life." Jason saw Benjamin's confused look and tried again. "He didn't stay dead, He just paid for it and then put out his hand to take it for me. All these years I've been hanging on to my sin, never knowing when it was going to blow up and kill me. When Mckilligin came to talk to me, he showed me how lame that was to keep hanging on to it. I gave it to Jesus and told Him I believed that He had died for my sin and came to life again, and that I was going to serve Him because of..." Jason looked up, searching for the right words. "Because I was thankful for what he did."

They stood silently, watching the police packing up the floodlights.

"Does that make sense?" Jason asked uneasily.

Benjamin nodded slowly. "Yeah, I think so."

"That's why I didn't shoot Jarris. Mckilligin has been telling me about how people who belong to Jesus are to act. He said they are not hateful toward their enemies, that they treat them the way Jesus would have if He was in their shoes. I guess He would be kinder or something. Since I was forgiven so much, I'm supposed to forgive, too."

Benjamin nodded again.

The lights of a car fell across them and both instinctively braced themselves. Benjamin stepped back and pulled out his gun, keeping it in Jason's sharp shadow.

Jason shaded his eyes against the light. The car oozed closer and they backed out of the way. When the driver's door was even with them Jason rapped on it with his knuckles. The window slid down.

"Taroe?"

Taroe tipped his hat chauffer style. "At your service."

"What are you doing here?"

Taroe leaned over to the passenger seat and picked up a

packet that was laying on the seat.

"Who is he?" Benjamin hissed skeptically.

"He's an FBI agent," Jason whispered back.

"You got the FBI on your side too?" Benjamin was impressed.

"He sort of came with the deal."

"So it seems." Taroe smiled patronizingly. "Here."

"What is it?" Jason asked, not moving to take the packet Taroe offered him.

"Your next mission." Taroe was amused by Jason's surprised look, but he retained his professional air.

"What do you mean?" Jason took the packet.

"It's your mission, Jason. That is if you will take it."

Jason nodded slowly, "What else is there to do?" A grin crept across his face.

Holding out a set of keys, Taroe smiled back. "Then this is yours."

Jason frowned, confused.

"No way! You get a car!" Benjamin's eyes lit up, and he shoved his gun back into his holster. "This is way cool!"

Jason took the keys, still too overwhelmed to speak.

"Most of your father's investments belonged to your family, and I took the liberty of transferring those to your name. You'll have to sign a few papers to make it official, but overall it is taken care of. He also had some other assets that will be placed into your account. The funds he received while working with the brothers, and a few other similar enterprises, had to be confiscated by the state. I figured you would understand."

Jason nodded. "So the car's from him?"

Taroe shrugged. "You could put it that way. In reality it is what would have gone to you if your father had passed away."

"I wish he had. It would have been easier," Jason muttered.

"I understand," Taroe told him gently. "But there is a

reason it happened this way."

"You sound like Joe," Jason told him. "He's in control."

"Who?" Taroe looked confused. "I was referring to the fact that, because of your involvement, we were able to catch some people we have been after for several years."

"Oh." Jason looked down at the keys in his hand. "I'm new to this whole faith thing, but Officer Mckilligin told me God has a better view of what's happening than we do down here."

Taroe looked thoughtful for a moment then nodded slowly. "It makes sense."

Benjamin, who had been standing by quietly, moved in as the conversation between them died down. "So, what kind of car is it?" he asked nonchalantly, resting his arm on the top of Taroe's car.

"A Mustang," Taroe told him.

"Nice." Benjamin's voice was full of admiration.

Taroe motioned with his head toward the back seat. "Climb in and I will take you to it."

Benjamin pushed Jason toward the back door. "You heard the man, get in."

Jason obeyed silently, clutching the keys as if they were the only link to his past. Benjamin ran around and climbed in the other side. He was doing a poor job disguising his excitement as he met Jason's eyes. "Mission accomplished, let's roll."

STRENGTH OF SILENCE

Eddie stayed where he was, listening. In the distance, a motor started up. He waited until it had faded before he stood. Dizziness washed over him, and he steadied himself against the counter. Still moving unsteadily, Eddie removed the floorboards and laid them aside. He heard something out front and froze. If the police caught him here, there would be no end of trouble. Moving toward the back door Eddie pushed it open. Outside, trash cans and a variety of other things littered the yard. A car motor rumbled toward him, and Eddie ran.

ROPER RETURNS

Jason Roper's second mission is clear-cut. He moves in with confidence, feeling invincible and unstoppable. But things are not what they appear on the surface. Even his invincibility has limits Roper did not know.

With no one to turn to, Roper finds himself sinking into a darkness he does not have the power to evade.

The Man Behind The Melody

The unexpected death of his twin sister threw Mark into a whirlwind of change. Disowned by his stepfather, Mark set out with only one goal in mind, to get as far away from the hateful man as possible. He clung desperately to the last link with his sister, her saxophone. Wandering the streets, Mark's path crossed with a stranger who could see potential no one else could see. Mark, an unwanted orphan, was offered the chance to become more than he had ever dreamed. But could the stranger be trusted?

Carbon
An Unforgettable Adventure

Carbon slipped out of bed and turned on the light. Taking a sheet of thick drawing paper from her desk she drew the face of the man the article simply called Roper. Pulling the picture she had drawn earlier from her file box, she laid them side by side on the desk. It was little or nothing to go on. The prisoner could have been a thousand different people. She had no face to compare. Suddenly the image of the stranger in the alley came to mind and Carbon frowned thoughtfully. He was the only one who would know.

THE SWORD OF JUSTICE

His mission was to eliminate those who had received the death penalty from the king. Justice was a King's Man. A man who had sworn allegiance to the king and who was backed in power by the full authority of the king himself. A man hated by every criminal in the king's realm.

Would Justice's loyalty to the king and skill with a sword be enough to protect him from his enemies?

THE STRIKER OF CHOI

The health of the Striker is the health of Choi. If he goes hungry, the town of Choi will grow hungry. If he is injured, the townspeople will suffer injury. He must be protected at all costs and must never leave the town of his birth. If he were to leave, the curse of the town would be in the hands of strangers.

Striker knew the legend well, but was there more to the legend than he had been told?

In Visible Fear

Billy dropped back on the bed, flickering between the visible world and the invisible. His breathing was rapid and irregular.

"Keep quiet, Billy, and I'll do my best to keep them off your trail. They were asking about you today."

"Don't let them find me." Again, Billy grasped the man's shirt, terror in his eyes.

The dark man pried his fingers open and stepped away. "You keep your mouth shut, I'll do what I can."

Taken by the Deep

"Must be a storm." Jeremy tried to sound confident.

"It's not a storm, Jeremy." Lydia's face was white and her voice faded into a whisper. "Please, you've got to let me go."

They didn't seem to hear her. Their eyes were riveted on the swirling water before them. It rose slowly as if the waves were standing, then moved forward with hypnotic swiftness.

Lydia screamed as the waters dove toward them. The salty spray wrapped around her, wrenching her from their grasp and pulling her into its depth.